Nantucket Jubilee

A Nantucket Sunset Series

Katie Winters

Chapter One

Autumn 1998

The Copperfield House's interior remained precisely the same after Bernard Copperfield was sent to prison. Photographs of Quentin, Alana, Julia, and Ella from many stages of babyhood, childhood, and awkward pre-teen and teenager eras adorned the fireplace and the walkways. A calendar continued to hang in the kitchen with February 1997's picture of a snowman on a Nantucket beach. Holidays came and went without any holiday decorations to acknowledge the passing seasons. It was eerie, or so Ella's friends told her when they came over. It was as though she lived in a haunted house.

Eighteen-year-old Ella carried a bag of groceries through the foyer, careful not to step on the floorboard that creaked. Upstairs, the television Greta had moved to the bedroom she now slept in alone produced a soft hum. It was rare that

1

Greta ever left that bedroom. Ella could count on one hand the number of times they'd eaten meals together at the kitchen table. The dining room, of course, had been abandoned, as it had been the natural meeting place for the entirety of the Copperfield Family, plus any artists, writers, or musicians who spent time at The Copperfield House's artist residency.

Just as she always did, Ella had shopped for enough groceries to keep herself and her mother alive for another week. Greta hadn't set foot outside the bounds of The Copperfield House since Bernard's trial. It was clear that Greta was a prisoner, just as much as Bernard was.

Ella lined up the groceries on the counter: orange juice, milk, a box of cereal, dry pasta, pasta sauce, slices of cheese, a loaf of bread, and mayonnaise. Once upon a time, the kitchen at The Copperfield House had been well-stocked with French cooking essentials. Garlic bulbs had been found in every nook and cranny. A permanent bowl of oranges had sat on the counter. Fine French wine had always been available for a quick pour. Unfortunately, Ella was no cook. Her talents were music-based only. Naturally, there had been a great deal of cereal in the past year and a half. Ella had no intentions of fixing that.

"Hello?" A beautiful yet very soft voice breezed in from the foyer.

Ella leaped to the doorway to find her best friend and bandmate, Stephanie. Stephanie loosened her backpack from her shoulder and eyed the thick dust that lined the baby grand piano.

"Hey, girl. Perfect timing. I just got back from the store," Ella said, beckoning Stephanie into the kitchen.

Stephanie entered and lifted herself up on the counter so that she could swing her legs. "Mr. Jenkins was looking for you after school."

"Oh?" Ella had raced out of last period to hit up the grocery store.

"Yeah. I told him you'd left already. He asked me to tell you to come and find him tomorrow," Stephanie explained.

Ella groaned as she opened the fridge and placed the milk and orange juice on the shelf within the door. "He's sent three letters home with me for Greta to sign."

"Has she seen them?"

"No way. I wouldn't do that to Greta. I learned how to do her signature years ago," Ella explained.

"Maybe he caught on to you," Stephanie said.

"God, I hope not. I mean, come on. Am I really going to need to do Calculus when the band gets famous?" Ella asked.

Stephanie wrinkled her nose. There was always hesitation in their conversation when Ella talked about pushing their band into the big leagues. Ella wasn't sure where that came from. To her, becoming a musician was the only way forward. On top of it all, her family was basically dead in the water. She hadn't heard from either of her sisters nor her brother in many months. There was no way on earth she would stick around Nantucket, waiting for something to happen to her. She was ready to go out there and make it happen for herself.

There was the sound of someone creaking up the front porch steps. Ella stepped out of the kitchen to watch as the mailman retreated, adjusting his mailbag across his shoulder. In the kitchen, Stephanie flicked on the local radio station, which played 1998's song of the summer, "Cruel Summer," by Ace of Base. Now that it was October, summer seemed so far out of reach. Even the memories were foggy now.

The mailman had left three bills— the phone bill, the television bill, and the heating bill. Because Ella now had Greta's signature down pat, she often took care of these things with a flourish of Greta's name at the bottom of a check book.

Beneath these three bills sat another envelope that was

3

smaller, with sharper corners. Ella flipped it over to discover Bernard Copperfield's beautiful handwriting. In the center, he'd written:

The Copperfield House.

Ella's heart thudded powerfully against her ribcage. It was almost too easy to imagine him in his prison clothing, the fabric of his sleeves rolled up to his elbows as he looped "The Copperfield House" across the envelope. This was the seventh letter he'd sent since he'd been sentenced to twenty-five years in prison. The first three had sent Greta into a downhill spiral of an ominous depression (one far worse than her typical "eat and sleep in front of the television" stasis). Since then, Ella had done her best to hide the letters— usually not opening them herself.

Back in the kitchen, Stephanie poured herself a bowl of cereal and chatted about another member of their band. Brenda played bass and had recently gotten into a tiff with another girl in school because they liked the same boy. Ella wasn't entirely sure what the deal with this guy was. To her, he seemed like just another Kurt Cobain wannabe with a messy haircut and ratty jeans.

"But Brenda is depressed," Stephanie said as she dug through the cereal to find the little bits of marshmallow. "Today, she talked about this gig in a dive bar in NYC. Her brother invited her there this weekend, maybe even to play bass in his band. But she thinks she's too sad."

Ella's ears lifted. "A gig?"

Stephanie shrugged. "I mean, you and I both know that Brenda isn't the greatest bass player in the world. But she isn't bad or anything. She can hold a beat. That's sometimes all a band really needs."

"But we should all go," Ella heard herself say. Her voice was a bit tenser than she'd expected it to be. "I mean, the gigs

4

around Nantucket are lame in comparison to anything in New York City."

"Sure."

"And if Brenda's brother knows the other bands involved, then we could probably get a slot," Ella continued, speaking quickly.

Stephanie's eyes were clouded. "You mean you think that we should run off to New York City and play a gig?" She said it as though it was the most ridiculous idea in the world.

"Why not?" Ella stopped herself from rolling her eyes. "You and Brenda can just tell your parents that you're sleeping here. Greta never checks up on me on the weekend. Or ever, really. She probably won't even know I'm gone. Besides, I'm eighteen, aren't I? The time to do this stuff is now."

Stephanie scrunched her nose. "It's Brenda's thing. Talk to her."

"But you'd be in?"

Stephanie shrugged and crunched through her cereal. Ella splayed the bills across the kitchen table and pocketed the letter from her father. Then, she reasoned that Greta hadn't eaten anything at all that day. As it was now four-fifteen, it was time to boil a pot of water and demand Greta eat at least three fork-fuls of pasta.

As Ella boiled the water and heated the sauce, Stephanie called Brenda to discuss the potential plan of heading to NYC for the "gig." Ella hissed questions to Stephanie as they spoke over the phone, like, "Could your brother get us a thirty-minute slot?" and, "Do you know if any agents will be there?" Brenda didn't have much in the way of answers. What she did have, just then, was a "oh, what the heck" attitude, which led her to convince Stephanie that this was the only way to live.

"We're rock stars, Stephanie," Brenda practically screamed over the phone so that Ella could hear it. "This is what rock stars do."

Ella tiptoed up the staircase to her mother's bedroom. The blue glow of the television illuminated the curve of her mother's nose and outlined her toes, which stuck out on the other side of the comforter. On television, a movie called *The Apartment* played for the fourth time that week.

"Hi, Momma." Ella stepped over a pile of clothes and placed the bowl of pasta on the bedside table. On one end of her mother's closet, her father's clothing still hung, as though he was just on a work trip and would return soon. Just once, Ella had asked her mother if she would consider getting rid of that stuff. Twenty-five years was a terribly long time. Ella wanted to give her mother space and time to move on.

Perhaps another dashing gentleman would come into Greta's life and make her forget her sorrows. Ella prayed for this, despite the fact that it broke her brain to think it. For the entirety of her life, Greta and Bernard had been the world's greatest and most loving couple. Everything they'd done, they'd done with respect, with artistry, and with hope for a brighter future.

Then why had Bernard stolen all that money from his colleagues and friends?

Had he really wanted to head off and build a new life with some other woman?

Even a year and a half after Bernard's trial, gossip still crept across the island like a parasite. As his youngest and only left-behind child, Ella received the brunt of the attacks surrounding Bernard's trial. Many of her classmates were in some way connected to the people he'd stolen from— and they poured all that hatred onto her.

Ella had considered dropping out of school, of course. But what were her other options? Quentin and Alana had both been out of the house by the time the accusations had begun. Julia had run off with her high school sweetheart, Charlie, and subsequently gotten her GED. Although Charlie had left Julia in the city and returned to the island to care for his ailing mother, it was rumored that Julia had already shacked up with someone new.

It was poisonous to think about just how little Ella knew about her siblings. Rage about that often filled her stomach. She wasn't always sure who to be angry with about that, though. She couldn't fully blame her siblings for leaving. Perhaps she would have done the same.

That said, a phone call here and there wouldn't have hurt. Ella did always make sure the phone bill was paid for that reason alone. Still, the only people who seemed to ever call were Ella's teachers, who were worried about her performance, plus Stephanie and Brenda, Ella's only friends in the world.

Greta didn't make a peep about the pasta. She continued to stare at the television screen. A final time, Ella said, "Remember to eat it soon, Momma. It'll get cold if you don't." She then walked slowly down the staircase and returned to the kitchen to find Stephanie digging through another bowl of cereal. Ella wanted to protest and tell her friend that that box of cereal was supposed to last her an entire week, but she kept her lips shut.

After Stephanie headed back home to meet her family for dinner, Ella cooked herself a bowl of pasta and sat with Bernard's letter. A part of her wanted to read it if only to dig back into the gorgeous texture of her father's mind. To her, he'd always been the greatest of all geniuses and often creative to a fault. The bedtime stories he'd told her back in the old days had kept her awake at night with their mysticism and their magic.

My darling Greta,

I've given up all hope on you believing my version of the truth. From within the walls of this prison, I know only that everyone comes here for a reason— and that God has put me here for the reason that I will spend the next twenty-three and a half years finding out.

It's not all bad, I suppose. My cellmate is here for another seven years. Fraud. He tells me funny stories about his life working for the stock exchange, where he rolled in money as a sort of pastime until someone at the firm figured out what he was actually up to. I asked him whether or not he would take it all back if he could. His answer surprised me. He said that out in the real world, he took everything for granted. He'd watch a sunset and think, "I wonder how much money I'll make tomorrow." He said he was filled with the worst sort of poison because it made him endlessly hungry for whatever he could get next.

Now, he says that he feels every minute of every single day. He's taught himself three languages since he got here five years ago, and he has a few more languages on his to-do list. When he leaves here, he says he wants to adopt a dog and roam the woods.

Anyway. It's fascinating learning how people were "before" and the plans they have for "after." It's certainly given me time to reflect about my own "before."

I like to think that I loved you as best as I could. I like to think that I kissed you enough, that I held you enough, and that we sang enough songs deep into the night. I like to think that we raised beautiful, kind, and creative children.

But the fact is— I'm here. I'm in prison. And again, I'm reckoning with the fact that I must have made a misstep along the way.

For the first year or so, I dreamed only of Nantucket and of your face. Bit-by-bit, the dreams are getting foggier. I'm so fearful that I won't be able to see your face for years on-end. It keeps me up at night before I then fall into the most heinous nightmares.

I must go. To end this letter, all I can say is that I love you. I love you with every ounce of my soul. And I count down the days until I see you and our darling children again.

Yours forever,
Bernard Copperfield

Chapter Two

"You guys, we made a wrong turn!" Brenda howled from the backseat of Stephanie's clunky car. The map was stretched out across her thighs, and her blue hair reflected starkly in the rear view mirror.

"Seriously?" Stephanie sounded frantic. Her hands clutched the steering wheel so powerfully that her fingers were white. Around them, New York City traffic bumped along, clearly uninterested in the fact that three teenagers from Nantucket hadn't a clue how inner-city traffic worked.

"Calm down." Ella collected the map from Brenda's lap and inspected the route they'd made that morning before ditching school after fifth period. "We just missed the turn. If you turn right up here, we can swoop back around and find that street again."

"Oh my God. We're going to die," Stephanie groaned.

"Will you stop that?" Ella snapped. "Look around you, Stephanie. Seriously. Look!"

"I can't look! I have to watch traffic, Ella!"

But at the traffic light, Stephanie allowed herself to turn her head from side to side to take in the splendorous views of downtown Greenwich Village, an artistic haven in a chaotic city so far from home. It was now seven-thirty at night, and the city had flung itself open for a dramatic night of art, music, fine restaurants, copious drinks, and lots of trouble. Ella wanted to lap up every moment of it, especially because it was so unlike her ordinary life. This was the daydream she used to get her through her life at The Copperfield House— yet here it was, right in front of her. She was living it.

It was a struggle to find a parking place close enough to the music venue. Even then, they had to pool together their cash to pay for it. As Stephanie clicked quarters into the parking meter, she muttered, "Brenda, your brother better let us play tonight."

Brenda kicked the curb sadly. "He said it was a maybe. There's no guarantee. I told you that."

"That's better than what we normally have to work with," Ella reminded them. "Normally, we're just stuck playing in my practice room. We need a real audience! We need real ears to hear what we've been working on all this time!"

The corners of Brenda's lips curved into a smile. Ella grabbed her guitar from the trunk and watched as Brenda adjusted the strap of her bass case over her shoulder. They hadn't bothered with a drum set, thinking that Stephanie could just use whatever set the venue had.

The Greenwich Village venue was called "The Toast." According to Brenda's older brother, The Toast was where all the punks and indie music kids hung out on the weekends. According to legend, Green Day had performed there when they had just been coming up on the scene.

From the outside, The Toast looked like any other dive bar. It was shadowed and dank looking with graffiti on the door and had only one window. Several twenty-somethings stood outside the bar, smoking cigarettes and chatting in a way that made them look very bored but also very cool. As Brenda, Stephanie, and Ella approached, Brenda's brother stepped out of the bar and placed a cigarette between his lips.

"Well, well, well. I can't believe you really made it," said Brenda's brother, Chris. Ella had always thought he was a terrible musician and an even worse person. He gave Brenda a half-hug and nodded at Stephanie and Ella, who he probably thought of as little kids. "Sneaking off the island for a bit of city action. Ella, Brenda tells me that you can really slay that thing."

Ella wanted to roll her eyes but decided against it. "Are we in for tonight, or what?"

Chris pressed his palms against his thighs. "Just be patient, little girl. I'll get you a slot sometime tonight. I'm in with the guy who makes the schedule. I can't promise you any longer than twenty minutes, though."

Ella told herself that twenty minutes would have to be enough. "Okay. Thanks."

They entered the bar behind Chris. The guy at the door who was there to check everyone's IDs didn't bother to glance at them at all. They passed the bar counter, where a woman in a belly shirt talked to an older guy with her hand on her hip. In the corner, a couple made out passionately despite the earliness of the hour. It was difficult for Ella to imagine what kind of world existed beyond the confines of Nantucket Island— yet here it was. Was she ready for it?

Backstage, Chris showed them where they could put their instruments and hang out before their gig. There were plenty of beer bottles on a table, along with bags of chips and pretzels. Two twenty-something guys with bad tattoos talked to one another in the corner and managed to ignore the pack of teenage girls altogether.

"The first concert is at eight," Chris explained. "You can either hang out back here or in the crowd, but don't get yourself into any trouble. If Mom finds out, she'll kill me." He eyed Brenda knowingly. He then glanced toward Ella to say,

"Although I guess if you got into any trouble, it would just be par for the course in that family of yours."

Ella's jaw dropped with surprise. Chris snickered to himself and hustled out of the back room, leaving Ella with her hands in fists.

"What the..." Stephanie's eyes widened. "Brenda, your brother is a piece of work."

Brenda rolled her eyes and placed a tender hand on Ella's shoulder. "You okay, hun?"

Ella shuddered. "Yeah. Fine." She sniffed. "As long as we get to play, I don't care what that guy says. We're here, aren't we? We made it."

Stephanie, Brenda, and Ella shared a secretive smile before stepping back out into the crowd to watch the first band. The band was made up of five guys on the early side of their twenties. They played bad punk music and hardly stayed on beat. Ella mostly rolled her eyes throughout the entire performance, uninterested in guys who only did the whole "music business" thing because they wanted to pick up chicks.

Brenda and Stephanie, on the other hand, jumped up and down throughout this performance and the next. Ella was mystified. *Didn't they hear just how bad this band sounded? Were they on the same page when it came to music? Or were* Brenda and Stephanie just the only girls in Ella's grade who cared about music at all?

Being eighteen was difficult for many reasons. Most of all, though, Ella felt as though she hovered between two realities. There was her time at The Copperfield House, with her family and her best friends in the band, but then there was this other life that awaited her wherever it was she ended up going. That big-time music career was somewhere out there. But she had to be patient on her quest.

The fourth band who stepped up on stage was yet another

four-piece of guys. Ella muttered into Stephanie's ear to say, "It's like there are no girls who can actually play around here."

The first chords of a punk song began to play. Stephanie called out over the sound. "Brenda's brother said that girls are supposed to be in the crowd, not on stage."

"That's so stupid!" Ella screeched.

But on stage, something strange was happening. While three of the band members seemed dull and boring, playing through the same-old chords and beats of a punk song, the drummer was extraordinary. He seemed to take full advantage of the entirety of the drums, whipping from one end to the other in a streamline. The other musicians couldn't hold a candle to him.

To top that off, the drummer seemed a little bit younger than the others, perhaps nineteen or twenty. As far as Ella could tell, his arms and legs showed off no tattoos. He wore the slightest of beards, little more than a five o'clock shadow, and he wore a black t-shirt without any allegiance to any other bands. His hair was black, as were his eyes, and he seemed to hover above the rest of the crowd in that music venue. It was as though he already belonged in a better one.

When the band's first song cut out, Ella lifted up on her tippy-toes and whispered in Stephanie's ear. "That drummer is really good."

Stephanie arched her brow. "You think?"

Again, Ella was flabbergasted that Stephanie hadn't noticed. But before she could explain just what she felt about his drumming techniques, the band surged into another song, then another. Throughout, Ella was wrapped in a daydream of watching him work his magic.

About twenty minutes later, Chris burst through the stage to tell the girls that they were "up next." Ella's throat tightened with excitement. The three of them hustled backstage to collect their things and compose themselves. In the room where the concert was, the band with the incredible drummer cut out, and the crowd roared.

"They left the room with good energy," Ella said, her confidence building. "I think we've got this."

"Oh my gosh. I'm so nervous," Brenda breathed.

But there wasn't time to be nervous. Already, the band with the drummer entered backstage, flipping their sweaty curls and dropping their guitars back into their cases. The drummer arrived last and shoved his drumsticks into his back pocket. He spoke to his bandmates and said, "Does anyone know who's up next?"

"Um. We are." Ella heard herself volunteer this information with a quivering voice.

The drummer's eyes dropped toward the three teenage girls in front of him. Ella's instinct was that he would immediately burst out laughing at the absurdity of them. But instead, he gave her a firm nod and said, "Good luck out there. There's a little bit of reverb. Be careful."

"Thanks for the tip," Ella returned. She then strutted out toward the stage with Brenda and Stephanie hot on her heels. She had to play the part of an arrogant rock star, even if she didn't necessarily feel like one. *That was the trick to everything,* she thought. *Just act the part.*

Ella, Stephanie, and Brenda hadn't played much more than a few Nantucket music festivals, a neighborhood association party, house parties for Nantucket locals, and a summer party that had gone south (namely because of an incident between Brenda and the guy she crushed on hard). Up on stage at The Toast, Ella's fingers and toes sizzled with the intensity of the crowd's noise. *Could they actually do this? Had they actually practiced enough?*

The crowd soon realized that the people on stage were teenage girls and quieted out of sheer curiosity. Ella knew they all expected them to have no talent and no stage presence. She was more than willing to prove them wrong.

"A-one. A-two. A-one, two, three!" Ella counted them off, and in a flash, they were off to the races on their first track. They were rock with a bit of indie flair and a decent amount of punk attitude. This brought Ella all over the stage as she howled and shredded her guitar, singing lyrics that she'd scribed in her bedroom during the most miserable year of her life— the year her father had been taken away.

The set lasted twenty-five minutes, longer than any they'd ever played. It was clear after the first song that they'd won the crowd over. By the time they finished, the crowd roared and screamed, calling out, "Yeah! Girls rock!" which sounded so silly and also so genuine in these strange moments. Ella was soaked with sweat, as were Stephanie and Brenda. Quickly, they met in the middle of the stage and shared a group hug before they gathered their things and hustled off.

Backstage, Ella drank two glasses of water and listened as Stephanie and Brenda geeked out about how good it had felt to be up there. The other guys in the room eyed them curiously, clearly impressed. In truth, Ella searched for just one person's approval.

And very soon, he appeared.

The drummer from the band who'd performed before them flashed through the back door and appeared before her, his hair disheveled every which way. They stared at one another for a long, frozen moment as the rest of the people backstage buzzed around them.

Finally, he spoke. "You were insane up there."

"Right back 'atcha."

His smile was crooked and endearing. As he took another step toward her, the sound of her heartbeat became a roar.

"I'm Will," he told her.

"Hey. I'm Ella." Did she sound cool? Like a cool "rock

chick"? Or did she sound like a dumb teenage girl from Nantucket Island?

"Who taught you how to play like that?"

Ella laughed, surprised at the question. "I taught myself."

Will snorted. "Gosh. Most of the guys in this place taught themselves as well. The only difference is, they suck, and you don't."

Ella refilled her glass of water, suddenly terrified that she would have nothing else to say after that. But before she could drum up another question or comment, Will asked, "Do you want to step outside with me? It's so hot in this bar."

Ella glanced toward Stephanie and Brenda, who were already fully aware of her conversation and gave her little, quick nods that told her they understood what she needed to do. Ella grabbed her coat and then followed Will back through the throng of concert-revelers and into the crisp October night. Out there, Will fumbled a cigarette from his pocket and told her that he really hated the habit. He planned to quit soon.

"Why don't you just quit now?" Ella asked with a sly smile.

Will guffawed. "That's a good question." He puffed his cigarette and grimaced. "I guess because everyone else in this city does it."

"Are you the kind of guy who goes along with the crowd?"

"I don't like to think so." Will's eyes glittered with intrigue. "You obviously don't live around here."

"Why is that so obvious?"

Will shrugged. "You're intelligent, for one."

"I'm sure there's someone in New York City more intelligent than I am."

"You're funny, for another," Will returned.

Ella's stomach twisted into a beautiful knot. There was no better thing than a handsome guy telling you that you were funny. Maybe this night was the pinnacle of her life.

"Where are you from, anyway?" Will asked, stomping out one-half of his cigarette. It was clear that he wasn't interested in it.

Maybe he wanted to kiss her. Maybe he didn't want to rule it out, at least.

"I'm from Nantucket," Ella said, choosing not to lie.

"Ah. Sweet. It looks beautiful there," he said.

"It supposedly is. I guess I'm just too used to it to realize it."

"That's the curse, isn't it?" Will asked.

They decided to head back inside to listen to another band. In the back, they howled in one another's ears about what they didn't like about these particular musicians. The next band was proof that this scene was just one bad musician after another. Eventually, Will grabbed them beers from the counter with his fake ID and led Ella into the corner so that they could talk more without the heinous parade of terrible punk songs.

Their conversation was already the most nutritional thing Ella knew. It seemed as though everything they said allowed another conversation to blossom. They spoke about music, their goals in the music world, and whether or not they really thought it was possible to make a career as a musician. Both felt that they owed it to themselves to try.

At some point, the bar began to clear out. Stephanie and Brenda appeared in front of Will and Ella's table; Brenda had her bass over her shoulder and looked prepared to go.

"Oh, Will. These are my bandmates," Ella said, her words slurring together after one beer. "Brenda and Stephanie."

Will shook their hands and said it was good to meet them. Brenda then announced that Chris wanted to head to a party a few blocks away.

"We kind of have to stick with him because we're staying at his place," Brenda explained.

Ella eyed Will, her heart darkening with disappointment.

Was this really the last time she would see Will? But a split-second later, Will removed his wallet from his back pocket, took out a small sheet of scrap paper, and scribed his number across it. To Ella's surprise, he then bent down and whispered, "I know of a better party. You can crash at my place. I'll sleep on the floor."

Ella gazed up to find her friends waiting for her. Something in her gut told her that this was what she had to do. Very subtly, she nodded her head and took the paper from Will's hand. She then handed it up to Stephanie and said, "Call this number tomorrow morning. I'll be..."

"Just around the corner," Will announced.

"Yeah."

"Ella, this is insane," Brenda said, her face marred with anger and fear.

Will leaped to his feet, removed his wallet again, and handed them his real ID, his library card, his Blockbuster card, and a few stubs from the subway. He began to tell them everything he could about himself— that his name was Will Ashton, that he had grown up "Up State," and that he was in the city to make it as a musician.

"I'm only nineteen," Will continued. "I just graduated from high school like five minutes ago. I've only had one girlfriend, and we broke up at the start of senior year. I didn't treat her badly or cheat on her; we just decided that we were better off as friends. Um. What else? I'm allergic to bees. I sometimes get car sick. I don't do drugs, and I hardly drink."

Stephanie and Brenda eyed one another, laughing nervously. Ella's heart nearly burst. Was this guy really doing all this to spend more time with her?

"If you can't track us down tomorrow, you can call my mother upstate," Will continued. "I'm from Albany. Her name is Teresa. Same last name."

"Teresa, huh?" Brenda smirked and tilted her head back

and forth. Her eyes locked with Ella's. "You promise that you're okay?"

"Yeah. I'm good, Brenda."

Ella shivered against Will, her heart bursting with expectation. Was she actually "okay"? Or was this the start of a story that ended with her "going missing"? That said, most of her family had "gone missing," one way or another. Nobody would miss her if she was gone.

Brenda and Stephanie each gave Ella a hug and then followed Chris out into the street. This left just Ella and Will in the shadows of the bar. More bar-dwellers hunkered in the corners and ordered additional beers. Ella's feet itched to just walk the streets that she didn't yet understand. She wanted to do it all alongside Will, this mysterious man who also seemed so familiar.

"Let's get out of here," Ella breathed.

Will and Ella bundled up in their autumn clothing. Ella wrapped her scarf around her neck and then adjusted her guitar over her shoulder. Meanwhile, Will banged his drumsticks against the cushion of the shoddy couch in a percussive tune that made Ella laugh. Her cheeks screamed with the pain of so much laughter. Since her father had left, she hadn't done a whole lot of it.

That night, Will and Ella wandered the streets of Greenwich Village like ghosts. They watched the Friday night revelers, giggled at their slurred voices and drunken movements, and occasionally paused to lean against smooth red bricks of townhouses and gaze into one another's eyes.

To Ella's surprise, it didn't take her long to explain the horrors of the previous year and a half of her life. The information just fell out of her, as though Will had deserved to know it all along. Will carried the news of her father's prison sentence, her mother's crippling depression, and her sisters' and brother's abandonment and laced his fingers through hers.

"When I saw you on stage tonight, I knew there was something to you. Something so unlike the other people who played," he began. "There was so much emotion in each of your chords and so much heartache in your lyrics. I thought to myself, I want to know what that girl is actually thinking."

Ella's voice was lost in her throat. It was as though, with the admittance of her family's situation, she'd run out of strength to say anything else.

Will's eyes glistened, as though he was on the verge of tears. A tear of Ella's own drifted down her cheek. It was a traitor. She didn't want to cry in front of this man! She wanted to be exceedingly cool. She wanted to seem like a city girl— not the heartbroken islander who'd driven so far from home.

"Sorry. I haven't ever talked about it to a stranger before," Ella explained.

The corner of Will's lips curved dangerously toward his ears. Gosh, he was handsome. It seemed almost illegal, like God shouldn't have allowed so much goodness to exist in one person.

"Does that mean I'm still a stranger?" Will asked.

"I guess it depends on your definition of 'stranger.'" Ella paused for a beat. "But I'd like to think you're a little bit more than a stranger."

"A little bit more than a stranger. That's a great review," Will teased.

Ella chortled. "Ask my friends. I don't give out compliments easily."

"Good," Will returned, his smile falling. "Giving out too many compliments just cheapens compliments in the first place. If you said everything was great, how could I actually know what you were thinking?"

Ella had heard her father, Bernard Copperfield, say something similar at the dinner table once. Her gaze fell to the ground.

Recognizing the change in mood, Will stepped closer to her and placed a tender hand over her ear. Ella's eyes returned to his. Across the street, an alarm began to blare. The sounds of the city were almost overwhelming, but they seemed to match the intensity of Ella's emotions.

"Are you okay?" Will whispered.

Ella nodded. With his face so close to hers, she couldn't imagine that anything else would go wrong for the rest of her life. Slowly, she lifted her chin so that his pillow-soft lips were mere inches from hers.

"I shouldn't kiss you," Ella rasped, still on the verge of tears.

"Why not?"

"Because I'll never see you again."

Will chuckled. "Why would you never see me again?"

"Because I want to too badly," Ella confessed. "People don't get what they want in life. Nothing ever works out the way we plan."

She knew this better than most. She was a Copperfield, after all.

But then Will whispered, "If you don't want to see me again, that's one thing. But I'd be open to the idea if you let it happen."

With that, Will closed the distance between them, his lips gently on hers. Ella closed her eyes and spun into the great abyss of wherever these feelings would lead her. Just then, she had to admit that she didn't care just what came next. For the first time in a year and a half, she felt the immensity of freedom. It wasn't half bad.

Chapter Three

Present Day

Will had left his toothbrush behind. Even three months after he packed his three bags and headed back to Manhattan, Ella still kept the bright blue toothbrush in the little cup by the sink. Now, on an impossibly dark and doom-filled night in August, Ella sweated at that very sink and dabbed at her armpits with squares of toilet paper. It was Friday, but it felt just like any other day, especially because Ella had shifts at both of her jobs over the weekend. It was almost impossible to make ends meet in Brooklyn. Perhaps it always had been— but things had gotten much more difficult lately.

Especially now that Will was gone.

Back in the living room, Ella's eighteen-year-old daughter, Laura, sat cross-legged on the couch with the remote control on her thigh. Laura waved a magazine toward her face to create a temporary wind. On the screen, Debbie Harry gave an interview about the craziest moments she lived through in the eighties. Back in the early two-thousands, even before Laura had been born, Ella and Will had spent a wild night of their own with Debbie Harry. Their indie rock band, Pottersville, had just toured across Japan and South Korea, and Debbie had just performed a show in Tokyo. One way or another, she'd heard of them, and they'd been invited to her hotel suite for champagne and whatever else came after that. The night was certainly on Ella's list of the craziest of her life, which was saying something. She supposed she would wait a few more years until she told Laura the extent of that story.

Just now, Ella was grateful to have her girl home for a little while longer. Very soon, Laura would move into the dorms at Columbia University and start her journey toward whatever came next. As Ella had just barely graduated high school and never bothered with college, she burst with pride over Laura's academic dreams. The girl had never been a musician, and both Will and Ella had been A-okay with that. (In fact, it had pleased them, as the money in the music world seemed to diminish by the day.)

"I'm glad I get you all to myself tonight," Ella said as she sat across the couch from her daughter.

Laura offered her a sweet smile. "Where's Danny tonight again?"

"Oh, he's over at Jason's," Ella explained. "He said something about a brand-new video game that he just had to play tonight. What am I going to do without you here in a few weeks? It'll just be me and a teenage boy."

Laura giggled. "I don't envy you."

"Gee. Thanks."

Ella hustled up to the kitchen and placed a bag of popcorn in the microwave. As the plate circled beneath the orange glow of the machine, Ella peeked out the window at the chaotic streets of Brooklyn on a Friday night. Now forty-two, Ella could hardly believe that the first time she'd come to New York City, she'd been Laura's age. She could still feel the big-hearted wonder she'd had for a city that seemed impossible to grasp. Now, the city seemed just as impossible, but she was often too tired to care.

Ella returned to the couch with a big blue bowl of popcorn and chatted to Laura for a while about the items they still needed to purchase for Laura's big move to college and the events planned with Laura's friends. Ever since Laura's girlhood, she'd been such a bright light of optimism, without any of the moodiness that had plagued Ella's youth. Ella had feared that with Will and Ella's separation, Laura would reveal the first "angst" of her teenage years. That hadn't happened, at least not yet.

In fact, Ella had always had a remarkably powerful relationship with her children. This had surprised Ella, as her relationship with her own family had been negligible since 1997.

Over the years, she and Will had toured the world to promote their albums. This had begged the question, *"What do we do with the children?"* With both of Will's parents gone, Ella had dropped her children off at The Copperfield House, of all places. Each time Ella had returned to The Copperfield House to drop off or fetch her children, fear had permeated through her body. It was really as though those horrific years in the nineties would always haunt her. Still, Greta had gotten a bit better since those first few years. Had she still been stuck in her bed for weeks at a time, Ella wouldn't have left her children with their grandmother. That was obvious.

It was nearly midnight. Ella's eyelids drooped ominously, proof that she needed to take her forty-two-year-old body to bed. She checked her phone and found another message from her sister, Julia, who now lived at The Copperfield House full-time.

JULIA: Dad's book comes out so soon. I'm literally freaking out.

Ella grimaced. Since both Alana and Julia had returned to The Copperfield House to rebuild their lives, they'd gotten incredibly chummy with one another. They'd told one another their deepest secrets and worked on healing after the extensive trauma of their past relationships. When Ella was around, Alana and Julia tried as hard as they could to include Ella in their sister squad. Ella, however, was resistant. How could she actually forgive her sisters for leaving her behind with Greta like that? Yes, it had been a long time ago. But Ella didn't forget so easily.

Besides, with Will gone and a bazillion bills to pay, it wasn't exactly a wonderful time for Ella to ask herself any deep questions about the Copperfield Family or spend time on Nantucket. Since that fateful night in Greenwich Village, Ella hadn't bothered to tell anyone her secrets, save for Will. This meant that each time she saw Alana or Julia at The Copperfield House, she kept her lips sealed to the horrific events of her own life.

Beyond that, she truly didn't want either of them to say what she thought they might: that Ella was so lucky that she and Will had never actually gotten married. *"Oh, it's so much easier for you,"* Ella could imagine Alana saying. *"Much less paperwork. You both can just move on from each other's lives."*

In some ways, this was true. Ella had to admit that. In others, her relationship with Will had been the only pillar upon which her entire life had rested. He had been her love, her best friend, her bandmate, her sounding board, her massage therapist, her nurse, her running partner, and her personal chef. Now, he was gone— and with his departure, the band had disintegrated, too.

Ella hadn't written a song in over three years. She hadn't

performed in over five. Music had been her lifeblood. Was that time of her life really over?

Ella's phone buzzed with an actual phone call, which was increasingly rare, with two teenagers and very few friends.

It was Will. Her heart pounded with fear as she lifted the phone. Maybe he called to have the talk they'd been neglecting all this time? Maybe he had decided that all this separation was silly and that they needed to get back to where they'd come from and write a gosh dang song?

"Hey." Ella's voice wavered.

"Ella, it's Will." His, on the other hand, was sharp and brash. "I'm at the hospital."

This was the breaking point. Ella blinked through the shadows of the kitchen and imagined the worst kinds of horrors.

"Danny's here," Will continued. "They're pumping his stomach."

Ella's jaw dropped. "Excuse me?" She didn't recognize her own voice.

"Just get down here," Will shot. "Brooklyn Hospital Center. I'll meet you in the waiting room."

The next three minutes passed in a flurry of near violence. Ella pushed her arms through the sleeves of a flannel shirt as Laura began to wail. Outside, Ella waved an arm in the air to hail a taxi, and within that taxi, she held onto Laura as Laura shook with sorrow. Throughout, Ella didn't allow herself to cry.

Once in the waiting room, Ella and Laura burst through the automatic doors to discover a war zone. It was a Friday in August in Brooklyn, NYC, and therefore, anyone who was anyone had had some kind of accident or mental breakdown. Babies wailed; mothers screeched with impatience; drunk men howled at their friends; and toddlers zoomed across the floor, unsupervised.

In the corner, Will sat on a plastic chair with his face in his hands. His legs were stretched out on either side of his torso like a basketball player's. Ella's heart shattered at the sight of him. This forty-three-year-old man was clearly broken with the news of their son. Ella wanted to hold him until the pain passed, just as he'd done with her countless times.

"Dad!" Laura got to him first. Will stood and hugged her with his powerful drummer's arms. Laura shook against him and burrowed her head in his chest. "What happened?" she wailed, although it was already clear. Danny hadn't been at Jason's playing video games. He'd been at an apartment party with older guys who'd pushed him to drink far more than his seventeen-year-old body allowed.

"Have you heard anything?" Ella tucked a brunette strand behind her ear and gazed into Will's eyes. He looked older and more tired than the last time she'd seen him on the day he'd moved out.

"Nothing," Will said, his voice curt. He then eyed Laura and said, "I have to talk to your mom for a little while, okay? Why don't you take my chair? We'll just head over to that hallway."

"Why can't you talk here?" Laura demanded.

"We just can't, sweetheart." Will's nostrils flared as Laura obeyed him and sat. "We'll be right back."

Ella followed Will blindly until they were out of sight of Laura. There, he turned on a heel and hissed, "What the hell happened tonight?"

Ella was suddenly terrified. He'd lost all sense of himself. "Will, I'm scared, too. Okay? Let's not make a scene."

"I thought you said the kids would be okay with you," Will shot back under his breath. "I thought you said that you could handle it."

"I can't be there with him every single minute of the day!"

27

Ella returned. "I can't hold his hand as he goes from place to place! He's seventeen."

Will groaned and pressed his hands over his cheeks, which stretched them out ghoulishly. Ella now remembered the millions of silly fights they'd gotten into over the past year or two. It was so not "them." She had no idea where the irritation had come from. One day, they'd woken up, and they hadn't been that couple any longer. The love just hadn't been enough.

"I'm just worried," Will breathed.

Ella's heart cracked at the edges. There was no way to tell yourself in the early days that being a mother would be the most painful experience in the world. Beautiful, but endlessly painful.

"He's going to be okay," Ella rasped, her throat tightening.

"How do you know?" Will countered.

Ella's head swam with rage. But before she could respond, Laura appeared. Her eyes were tinged with red, and her cheeks were blotchy and shining with tears. She raced toward the two of them, her mother and father, and forced them into a group hug. For the slightest of moments, Will placed his hand over Ella's. But in the blink of an eye, it was gone.

Chapter Four

"Oh my gosh. Dave Grohl was there? You're kidding, Dad." Laura leaned against the doorframe of the kitchen and chatted to her father on the phone. She seemed oddly nervous, with her foot propped up against the inside of the opposite ankle and her finger twirling her hair. Will had left on his first-ever tour without Ella about five days ago, yet had only bothered to call his children now. Probably, Laura felt like she had to prove something to him— that she was good enough to be missed.

Ella dried the last of the breakfast dishes and placed the plate gently in a stack with the others. *Don't put yourself through this*, she told herself, as she'd recognized her own emotional patterns. When she grew resentful of Will, everything else in her world seemed dark and dreary. That said, she wasn't entirely pleased that Will was allowed to just head off on tour with his brand-new band and hang out with Dave Grohl while she was left to pick up the pieces of their dead partnership and care for their children. Once upon a time, she'd been famous, too.

Ella left Laura in the kitchen and inspected the line of backpacks at the door, one for Ella, one for Laura, and one for Danny. That morning, they were headed to Nantucket Island for the opening party for Bernard Copperfield's newest novel, which Julia had decided to use as a "Hail Mary" for her struggling Chicago-based publishing house. Due to the success of Bernard's previous novel and his now-infamous reputation, pre-sales for the book, *The Time He Lost,* had reached insane numbers. Based on a recent phone conversation with Julia, she was terribly pleased. On the other hand, Bernard seemed not to care at all. "His moods shift so quickly. You never really know where his head is at. Sometimes, he's garrulous and eager to eat dinner with Mom, Alana, and I. Other times, he stays in his room for weeks at a time."

Much like his grandfather, Danny remained latched away in his room, blaring the Yeah Yeah Yeahs' "Maps." Ella recognized the severity of the song choice. It was clear that Danny remained ill and depressed in the wake of the alcohol poisoning incident. The hospital stint had been two grueling weeks ago, and still, Danny struggled to look Ella in the eye. Very soon, Danny would start his senior year at his high school there in Brooklyn, and Ella's stomach twisted with anxiety. Without Will there, she was unsure about how to wade through the terrors of handling a teenage boy with an alcohol problem.

Ella retreated to her bedroom to make sure she hadn't forgotten anything. Toothbrush, makeup, and other toiletries were all accounted for. In her flurry back out into the hallway, she glanced at the stack of paperwork on the bedroom desk— legal jargon that was supposed to separate Will and Ella in a very concrete way. There would be no more shared accounts or recognition from the government that they were a "unit." The language of the paperwork was dense and alienating. Several times over the previous two weeks, just reading the first paragraphs had made her weep.

"Danny? You want to talk to Dad?" Laura called down the hallway.

Danny's muffled, "No," came back.

"You sure? He's in Memphis with Dave Grohl."

"I don't give a crap about Dave Grohl," Danny called back.

The corners of Ella's lips curled into the smallest of smiles. She stepped into the hall and tapped at Danny's door gently. "Hey, honey. You about ready to hit the road?"

Danny opened the door slowly to reveal all six feet of him, his shoulders broad yet bony from his weight loss and his cheeks sallow. Based on his appearance, he looked hungover from either drugs or alcohol. This, Ella knew, was not true, as he'd spent almost the entirety of the previous two weeks in that very room. Ella and Will hadn't even "grounded" him. He'd simply known to ground himself.

"Um. Yeah." Danny splayed his fingers through his black locks and blinked into the light of the hallway with an expression that reminded Ella painfully of Will back in the old days.

Ella pressed a hand on Danny's shoulder. She wanted so desperately to say the "right" thing, whatever it was that would take the pain from Danny's eyes. *What had led him to drink so much? Was it the separation? His father's departure?* Or something uniquely "teenager" that Ella couldn't fully understand anymore, as she was too far away from those experiences herself?

"I packed some snacks," Ella said instead, removing her hand.

"Oh. Awesome." Danny sniffed and leaned back to turn off his speaker and retrieve his phone from his unmade bed. "Do you know if Aunt Julia's kids are coming?"

"I believe they are," Ella replied, grateful that Danny showed the slightest interest in her family.

Ella's older sister, Julia, had three kids: Anna, twenty-two, Henry, twenty, and Rachel, who was about to start her sophomore year at University of Michigan. It was remarkable that Ella and Julia's children had hit it off so well during their visits to Nantucket Island, especially given Julia and Ella's decades apart. Alana had no children, and Quintin's children were in that upper echelon of Manhattan-ites, which meant that they were inherently different from Ella's own children. Plus, Quintin wanted nothing to do with the Copperfield Family, which was all right with Ella. Quintin, who worked as a nightly news anchor in the city of New York, was well-recognized across the country, well-respected in the field of journalism, and generally unliked by the rest of the Copperfield siblings. This was life.

The drive from Brooklyn to Hyannis took approximately four hours and forty-five minutes. Throughout, Danny and Laura were seamless in their music choices, crafting a playlist that thrilled Ella with its commitment to many decades of music and many different genres.

"I have to say, I think your father and I handled your music education really well," Ella said, shimmying her shoulders.

Laura nibbled on a Twizzler in the front seat and said nothing. In the backseat, Danny ruffled his hands through his hair nervously. Maybe it was better not to talk about Will. Maybe her children weren't sure what to say; maybe they didn't want to hurt her or remind themselves of their own pain. Ella could understand that. Will had been the only person in the world she'd been able to open up to regarding her father's prison sentence, her siblings' abandonment, and her mother's depression.

You had to pick your words carefully in life. Ella knew that.

Nantucket Island spun with life. A hearty sun beat heavily in an eggshell blue sky, and tourists rushed across the road with panicked eyes, as though they'd forgotten any concept of "slowing down" and wanted to find a way to experience as much joy as possible, as quickly as possible. A little girl in the center of a crosswalk lost the top of her ice cream cone and blinked cartoonishly large eyes toward the ground as she wailed.

"I get it," Laura quipped. "Summer can be a heartbreaking time."

Ella chuckled. "There will be other ice cream cones."

"She doesn't want to hear that right now," Laura said. "She wants that one."

This conversation was clearly not about ice cream cones. It was about regret and sorrow and wanting a life you could no longer have. Ella bit down on her lower lip and then whispered, "Aren't you a poet, Laura."

Since April, Julia had flung herself full force into the repair of The Copperfield House. The once-dilapidated old Victorian home now stood re-painted and stately. Its shutters were thrown open to the gorgeous August day.

"It looks so good," Laura breathed as she pressed open the front door of the station wagon. "Worlds better than those summers Danny and I spent here."

"You got that right," Danny chimed in. "As a kid, I was genuinely terrified of whatever ghosts lurked in there."

"Me too," Laura admitted. "But I always tried to be brave for you."

"Ha. My hero," Danny mocked playfully.

"Who do I hear out there?" A gorgeous and stately Greta Copperfield appeared at the front door. Since Bernard's return in April, she'd gained probably fifteen healthy pounds and now stood tall and powerful, her cheeks flashing with pink and her legs muscular from long walks on the beach. She had no relation to the Greta of Ella's teenage years, the one Ella had had to cook and clean for.

"Grandma! Hi!" Laura scampered forward and wrapped Greta in a hug. Danny followed close behind and did the same.

"You look gorgeous, Gram," Laura complimented, stepping back to inspect Greta's red-and-while polka-dotted dress.

"Oh, this old thing," Greta said. "I pulled it out of the back of my closet."

"Vintage!" Laura cried.

Ella grabbed her backpack from the back trunk of the station wagon and followed her children up the porch steps. There, she fell into the warm embrace of her mother, who smelled of lilacs and sunshine with the faintest hint of salt from the sea.

"Oh, Ella." Greta leaned back and stitched her eyebrows together. "You look quite tired."

Ella scrunched her nose. "I'm fine, Mom."

"The city must be terribly stressful," Greta said. "Your sisters have really taken a liking to Nantucket. Why don't..."

"Uh oh." The iconic Alana Copperfield appeared in the downstairs living room with her hands on her hips. "Has Mom already started asking you to move to Nantucket? How long has it been, Mom? Thirty seconds? Forty-five?"

Greta waved a hand. "You can't blame me for wanting all my children back. I've gotten greedy."

Alana laughed and stepped forward to wrap Ella in a hug. "Don't blame her for anything she says. She's already had a mimosa."

Back in the kitchen, Julia's three children, Anna, Henry, and Rachel, sat around a big platter of pancakes. They leaped up to hug Laura and Danny and grabbed chairs and plates for them.

"Grandma has been spoiling us with these amazing, delicious meals," Anna explained. "I've only been here since Wednesday, and I swear, I've gained five pounds."

"There's no way," Greta quipped, a twinkle in her eye.

"Grandma, I saw how much butter you put in that gratin last night," Anna said with a cheeky grin.

"Americans are so afraid of butter!" Greta exclaimed. "The French never shy away from it. They lathered it on everything."

"How was your drive?" Alana tugged Ella's backpack from her shoulder and heaved it upon her own instead.

"It went quickly," Ella explained, her brain whizzing with input. "Where's Julia?"

"Oh, she's having a meltdown, as usual," Alana said with a chuckle. "Let's get your stuff inside and run over to help her out."

"Sounds like a plan," Ella returned.

The release party for Bernard Copperfield's second published novel was to begin at five o'clock later that afternoon. Julia and the event manager she'd recently hired for her newly revived publishing house had decided to throw the party in the residency space of The Copperfield House, which featured an immaculate library with large windows and doors that opened out onto the beach. This was the space where many of the previous Copperfield artist residents had shown off their work prior to departure. Ella could remember many intimate concerts, book readings, little plays, and painting displays between the old-world shelves.

In the library, Julia and her event manager, Valerie, hovered over several clipboards. Julia's hair was frizzy as she continued to run her fingers through it and worry herself to death about the party and its numerous guests, many of whom were coming from off the island.

"Jules," Ella said her name in singsong.

Julia lifted her gaze and opened her lips into an outrageous smile. In a flash, she crossed the room and threw herself into a three-person hug. There they stood, the three Copperfield Sisters, giggling madly at the sheer wonder of being back together again. Ella wondered if they would ever get used to it.

"You made it!" Julia howled.

"I did. And I heard you need help," Ella announced.

Julia scrunched her nose and broke her hug. "My to-do list is still a mile long. And on top of it all, I still need someone to go down to the post office to pick up all two hundred copies of Dad's book. We really, really need them tonight. Obviously."

"That's the whole point of the evening, Julia!" Alana chided.

"It's not my fault that the postal service delivered them late," Julia shot back. She then puffed out her cheeks and added, "I want everything to be perfect tonight. It's Dad's big return to the literary world."

"Any sign from the big man?" Ella asked.

Julia shook her head and glanced toward the other half of the house, where Bernard remained locked away in his study. "As recently as last month, he was really excited about seeing so many of his old colleagues in the literary world. But now, I think he's frightened that they've only come all this way to gawk at him."

"That's awful," Ella breathed.

"But it also might be partially true," Alana offered.

"Alana!" Julia cried.

"What? The entire world views Dad with morbid curiosity," Alana countered. "We're the only ones who know that he didn't actually take all that money. We can't blame everyone else for not getting it yet."

As Julia nodded knowingly, Ella's stomach tightened. It was clear that her sisters were still deep in the throes of proving Bernard Copperfield's innocence. But what good would it do? Bernard had already spent twenty-five years in prison. Their family had already lost all that time. Besides, Ella wasn't sure what she believed. Maybe Bernard had really wanted to steal all that money and escape the island with his probable mistress, Marcia Conrad. Maybe Alana and Julia just didn't want to believe it.

It was difficult to believe that the ones you loved could turn on you like that. But Ella knew that it happened all the time.

Chapter Five

A t five o'clock sharp, Ella stood just outside the entrance to the residency's library so that the breeze off the ocean swept through the skirt of her black dress and fluttered it prettily around her knees. From where she stood, she could just barely make out the curve of Bernard Copperfield's pipe outside of the window of his study. Smoke puffed toward the tip tops of the surrounding trees.

Within the library, Julia and her publishing team finished up the final touches on the space. Although Greta had wanted to prepare the food herself, Julia had insisted on catering the event, which was a decision that Ella respected. This party was to bring more people into The Copperfield House than had been in over twenty-five years. Greta would be anxious; it would only worsen things if she was in charge of the menu.

Danny stepped out into the soft light of the early evening with one of his grandfather's books tucked under his arm. He was dressed in a button-down shirt and a pair of nice jeans, which was about as fancy as it got with Danny.

"Hey, bud." Ella forced a smile. "Thanks for your help this afternoon with the books."

"These books are whoppers," Danny joked. "Seven hundred and sixty-seven pages?"

"Your grandfather was always very verbose," Ella tried. "I guess he had to put all those thoughts somewhere while he was in prison."

Danny's face was contemplative. "Aunt Alana said the book is all about Grandpa's innocence. That it's about an innocent man who feels so much regret about missing his life."

Ella's cheek twitched. "Your aunts have some theories about your grandfather's past."

"You don't believe those theories?"

"I just think we should all find a way to move on," Ella stuttered slightly. "And I don't know if digging up the past will help any of us. That's all."

Just then, Julia's voice carried from the heart of the library. "All right, everyone! People should be arriving any minute. Emerson, remember that you're in charge of social media. Post like your life depends on it."

Ella and Danny locked eyes and giggled quietly. They then entered the library to huddle beside Laura, who'd positioned herself directly next to one of the larger snack tables. Ella reached out to select a pretzel from a large tray. Julia's eyes widened angrily, which made Ella slowly bring her hand back to her side. She didn't want to anger the beast. Not tonight.

Julia continued. "Remember, the book goes on sale today across the country, but many people here tonight already received an advanced copy and have taken the time to discuss and review the book. Reviews are coming in— and they're spectacular. Let's make sure to be polite, entertaining, and excited about the future of Dad's career and The Copperfield House itself.

"This party is about more than a novel. It's about the

rebirth of The Copperfield House and our assertion that very soon, we will reopen it as a transformed artist residency. Already, Alana has begun that work with her acting seminars for teenage girls. But this is only the beginning of what will certainly be a remarkable chapter. And within that chapter, I know that my sisters and I will find the proof we need to show that Bernard Copperfield is innocent of the crimes he served time for. This book is only the first step."

Ella had to admit that she couldn't quite get up the energy to care about The Copperfield House's new residency program. Still, at the end of Julia's speech, she clapped along with her other family members and Julia's team, grateful for a distraction from her raggedy Brooklyn life.

One after another, guests began to arrive. Julia put Ella and Laura in charge of the front desk nearest the door, where guests checked in and received their goodie bags. Bloggers, book reviewers, and semi-famous literary faces appeared before the table, often peering through very thick glasses as they introduced themselves.

Once, Laura whispered into Ella's ear to say, "Your music friends are way cooler than these book types."

To this, Ella snickered and said, "Come on. Just because they don't wear leather jackets and love Iggy Pop doesn't mean they're not cool."

At this, one of the book reviewers in the growing crowd began to hiccup. Some wine spilled from his lips and stained his striped shirt. Laura placed her hand over her mouth and nearly burst with laughter. Ella rolled her eyes and stifled her own giggles.

"Have you seen your brother?" Ella asked Laura during a small break in the stream of guests.

"Uh. He was back there with Grandma," Laura replied, waving her pen back behind her shoulder.

Ella's brain fuzzed with worry. Around them, revelers

sipped wine and chatted about Bernard's book, their own literary accomplishments, and the state of the publishing industry. Ella had a terrible, flashing mental image of Danny mere hours after his alcohol poisoning. *Suppose he snuck off with an entire bottle of wine?* She would never forgive herself for not paying attention.

"I'm just going to check up on him," Ella muttered.

"Mom, I think he's okay," Laura offered, her eyebrows lowered.

"I have to make sure." Ella leaped up as another batch of guests approached the desk. She then wove through the haze of perfume and cologne and locked eyes with Julia across the library. Julia was in what looked to be a serious conversation with another woman who owned a publishing house. As the woman spoke, Julia mouthed, "Are you okay?" To this, Ella just nodded.

She didn't want her family to know about the inherent brokenness of her own family. She didn't want them to know that she and Will had separated. She didn't want them to know that Danny had been in the hospital. She didn't want them to know that she was hardly keeping herself together.

"Hey, Rach." Ella found her niece in the corner with her brother, Henry. Both ate cupcakes, and their lips were outlined with chocolate. "Have you seen Danny?"

"Oh, um. I think he was somewhere with Anna?"

"Any idea of where they ran off to?"

Rachel's beautiful face contorted. "They said something about going back to the main area of the house."

Ella's heart pounded. "Thank you, Rach." She then flung herself toward the hallway that led back toward the main house. Anna was twenty-two; Danny was seventeen, but a big-city seventeen, which made him far more "adult" than kids his age in small towns.

Out of view of the party, Ella sprinted down the hallway

and erupted through the door that separated the residency from the main house. Back in the old days of The Copperfield House, one half of the house had been the servants' quarters, while the other had belonged to the family who hired them. When Ella had been a child, she'd been told not to go into the residency half of the house without one of her parents. It had been essential to let the artists have their space, their time, and their quiet.

It was strange to feel all those separate worlds and stories spinning through the air of the newly revitalized home.

Ella flung open the door to the living room of The Copperfield House, where, to her incredible surprise, she discovered Danny, Anna, and their grandfather, Bernard Copperfield, seated at the bench in front of the baby grand piano. The three of them turned to glance her way, surprised at how chaotically she'd entered the room.

"Mom? Are you okay? You look freaked out," Danny said. He then lifted a glass of juice and sipped it evenly.

"Oh. Sure. Yeah." Ella tried to breathe normally and finally managed to smile at her father. "Hi, Dad." She stepped toward him and kissed the tiny piece of skin above the whiskers of his cheek. "Quite a party going on for you over there."

Bernard, who wore a flannel shirt and a pair of old jeans, chuckled knowingly. "Your sister stopped by my office this afternoon to ask me a final time to make an appearance."

"I take it you're not up for it?" Ella asked, surprised at how good it was to see his face again. Like Greta, he looked healthier than he had back in April.

"I've avoided those mean-spirited literary types for over twenty-five years," Bernard affirmed. "I don't need to go over there so that they talk my ear off about whether or not James Joyce is relevant in the modern age or blah blah blah."

Danny tossed his head back, cackling at his grandfather's joke. Even Ella felt herself smile.

"To be honest with you, I think the book will sell better if you don't go," Anna pointed out. "The fact that you're so elusive makes people even more interested in you and your story. People love a thing they can't understand."

"You have a point," Danny offered.

Bernard rolled his eyes back playfully and stretched his fingers across the keys. He then began to play, tinkling across the keys as he made up a song on the spot. "I don't give a damn about book sales. I don't give a damn about press."

Ella snorted. "Don't play too loudly. Someone over there is in charge of social media. If Julia gets wind of this, you'll be on a million phone screens in a split-second."

"I hardly understand what any of that means," Bernard said, his eyes twinkling. He then stopped his playing quickly so that the piano hummed in front of them. "That said, I do hope you're right, Anna. I know that Julia's publishing house is very important to her and that every book sale keeps our family going. And heck, we worked hard on editing that book this summer. I'm grateful that the book is out in the world. I'm grateful that people will read it and perhaps understand me if only a little bit. I just don't like the idea of hobnobbing and bootlicking. That's all."

Ella sighed and rubbed her stomach, which was clearly void of snacks from the food table. "I have to get back to the party. I left Laura high and dry at the guest table. You three take care of yourselves over here, okay?"

Bernard nodded and again flung into a piano tune. Danny sipped his juice and gave his mother a genuine smile. Perhaps Ella was wrong. Perhaps she didn't need to be worried about Danny. Perhaps that single hospital visit had been enough to put the fear of God in him for good.

Back at the party, Alana and Julia stood off to the side with raised wine glasses and chatted, their lips flashing open to reveal their white and perfect teeth. It was not lost on Ella that

Julia and Alana were more traditionally beautiful than she was. Sure, Alana was the ex-model of the family, but Julia had always been similarly stunning— just more bookish.

"Ella! Where's your drink?" Julia waved Ella over and squeezed her elbow as Alana fetched a glass of red wine from a passing server.

"The party seems to be going well?" Ella asked, holding the stem of her wine glass.

"Oh, better than I ever expected," Julia reported. Under her breath, she added, "I'm grateful for that gorgeous sunset. People are posting so much on their social media channels. There's a hashtag going around called #WhereIsBernard? Maybe it's better that Dad decided not to drop by."

Ella laughed inwardly, remembering what Anna had said little more than a minute before. "I think this would overwhelm him, anyway."

"You're right," Alana offered. "He's usually just over-whelmed by his family. An entire literary crowd would be too much."

"Oh my gosh! Ella Copperfield?" An unfamiliar voice rang out from the crowd. With the voice came a dark-eyed woman in a perfectly cut suit and a bob that scanned the tops of her ears.

"It's me?" Ella felt foolish and unsure.

The woman's smile was enormous. "To be honest with you, I was hoping you'd be here."

"I'm so glad?" Ella had no idea who this person was.

The woman stuck out her hand and shook Ella's. "My name is Bunny Grimm. I've been a music journalist with *Rolling Stone* forever."

"Oh!" Ella recognized that name. Bunny Grimm had stuck her neck out for Will and Ella's band, Pottersville, countless times over the years. Once, she'd even given one of their albums a ten-point rating, which was the highest-possible rating that the magazine offered. "Gosh, of course. I guess I haven't seen you in, what? Fifteen years?"

Bunny nodded. "So glad you remember. That party in LA, right?"

Ella's eyes widened at the memory of the iconic night where she'd met Dolly Parton and then sobbed drunkenly to Will about how it was the "best moment of her life."

"What are you doing here, Bunny?" Ella sputtered.

"Oh, I've started doing book reviews alongside music reviews," Bunny explained. "And your father's story has made this book a real hot commodity this season." She then turned toward Julia and said, "Congratulations, by the way."

Julia's cheeks burned crimson. "Thank you. It means a lot that people like you came for the release party."

Bunny continued to smile like a shark. She then turned her attention back toward Ella and said, "You won't believe this, but I'm off to Texas tomorrow to cover Will's tour. It broke my heart that you two broke things off."

It was as though Bunny had run through Ella with a knife. Her jaw dropped with surprise.

"I mean, your music was always spectacular. My favorite of the two-thousands," Bunny continued. "You and Will were a match made in musical heaven. But I guess not everything can last forever. I imagine that you'll start your own musical project here soon. It's an exciting chapter, really." Bunny hunted through her pocket and then handed Ella a business card. "You'd better call me when you get that new musical project up and running. I want to do a piece about you. It seems overly easy for a man to start over again after a band and relationship breakup. But a woman? I mean, you're like the modern Stevie Nicks. Our readers would be eager to hear all about it."

Soon after, Bunny ran off to chat with another journalist. This left Ella staring down at the business card, with both

Alana and Ella slack-jawed beside her. Softly, Julia cupped Ella's elbow and prepared to say something.

"Don't," Ella hissed, her eyes filling with tears. "Please."

With that, she hustled through the crowd to return to the front table with Laura. There, Laura handed her a pen and said, "There's a line around the porch. I couldn't keep up!"

Ella swept a finger beneath her eye to catch the lone tear. "Sorry, hon."

Laura paused, her pen hovering above the check-in sheet. "Are you okay?"

"Just fine." Ella lifted her chin to greet yet another literary figure, then said, "Welcome to The Copperfield House. We're so glad to have you here with us tonight."

Chapter Six

At eleven that night, The Copperfield House's very first party in twenty-five years came to a close. Bloggers, photographers, literary critics, and other writers who'd come to ogle Bernard Copperfield stepped out beneath the light of the moon and headed back to town, where inevitably, they'd join the throngs of tourists, drink expensive glasses of wine, and gossip about the party they'd just attended.

Julia was out on the porch having a last-minute meeting with her publishing house staff. Laura, Henry, and Rachel had all run off to find Anna and Danny back in the main house. Alana was in the corner chatting with her new sort-of boyfriend, Jeremy, and Julia's new boyfriend, Charlie. This left Ella weak in the knees and exhausted. She collapsed in a cushioned chair near the snack table, selected a cupcake, and dug her teeth into the cream cheese frosting. Her thoughts turned into a strange, inarticulate buzz.

The worst had happened. Ella's secret about her relationship with Will had been revealed. She hated that her sisters would want to talk about it. Ella had simply wanted to come home for a few days, support Julia's publishing house and her father's book, and then return to Brooklyn to prepare for the next era of her life. Very soon, Laura was off to college at Columbia University. Very soon, it would just be Danny and Ella, alone in that expensive apartment, as Ella struggled to pay the bills, and Danny fought his clear desire to drink himself into nothingness. She didn't need judgment from her sisters on top of all that.

Ella continued to nibble at the edge of her cupcake and slowly fell deeper into the chair. Somewhere in her mind, she caught Alana's voice, saying goodbye to several people. Then, Julia called a final, *"Be safe out there!"* into the night.

A split-second later, Ella was aware of the formidable presence of her two sisters, who stood on the other side of the snack table and peered down at her curiously. Ella forced herself back upright in the chair, careful not to get any frosting on her clothing. Both Julia and Alana looked on the verge of sobbing.

"Ella..." Alana began, her voice breaking. "Why didn't you tell us?"

Ella rolled her eyes back into her head.

"Seriously, Ella. You know about the year that Alana and I had. We're both going through divorces. My publishing house almost went under. My children hated me for not telling them that Jackson left me," Julia began.

"Come on. They didn't hate you. They were worried about you," Alana interjected.

Julia bristled. "Tensions were high. And it's not like I'm anywhere close to where I need to be. But I'm getting there! Bit by bit, I'm healing. And Alana is, too. Right, Alana?"

"Most days," Alana offered, her voice low.

Ella set her half-eaten cupcake on the edge of the snack table. Alana and Julia grabbed chairs and scooted around the table. In the silence, Alana poured them each a small glass of wine, and the three of them watched as the liquid rained down and darkened into a pool of dark red.

Ella held her glass and peered at her reflection in the liquid. Both Alana and Julia seemed heavy with disappointment. But how could Ella possibly explain to them why she didn't feel comfortable telling them about her private life?

Ella took a sip of wine. The cabernet trickled along her tongue in dark, woody tones with a hint of berries. Finally, she lifted her eyes toward her sisters and said, "I can't tell you how hard it was when everyone left."

Julia's cheeks tightened. They knew that Ella spoke of the time "after" Bernard's sentencing when Ella and Greta were left alone in that house.

"Ella, I'm so, so..." Julia began.

"Don't apologize. It doesn't change anything," Ella interjected. "I just need to explain. During that time, I felt like I had nobody. Mom never got out of bed. Like, never. I made almost every meal for her. I had to do the chores. I had to keep myself alive, even when everything felt so pointless. Back then, the only thing that didn't feel pointless was music. And one night, I snuck off to Manhattan with my high school band and played in a dingy nightclub for bad punk bands. That was the night I met Will."

Alana and Julia were captivated. Clearly, this was the sort of story you were supposed to share with your sisters.

"I found myself immediately opening up to him about our family and about Dad," Ella continued, her voice breaking. "There was such goodness to him. I knew he could handle everything about me, even the messiest parts. After graduation, I immediately moved to Brooklyn to be with him. And a split-second later, it seemed like we formed a band. The fame was such a surprise. I wasn't sure how to handle it. We traveled the country together, staying in crummy hotels or sleeping in the van. Sometimes, we talked about getting married. Other times, we laughed it off, asking ourselves why we needed some kind of 'proof' that we loved each other. During those years, The Copperfield House nightmare seemed like somebody else's life. And then, eighteen years ago, Laura came, followed shortly by Danny."

Ella sipped her wine and rolled her shoulders forward. She'd never told anyone the "story of her life" before, not like this. It felt strange to explain it all to her sisters. In some ways, her sisters were more like strangers than blood.

"It was so hard over the years to maintain the music schedule and raise children," Ella continued. "Sometimes, we struck a pretty good balance, but more often than not, we found ourselves rolling through time and space without any concept of gravity. I can't tell you when the love faded. Probably around the time we stopped making time to play music together. Probably around the time that Laura hit puberty and started fighting with us. Or, maybe, we just woke up one day and were completely different people."

"When did Will move out?" Alana asked, her voice breaking.

"We've been falling apart for about a year now. I asked him to leave in May."

Alana and Julia's jaws dropped.

"But we saw you so much over the summer," Alana said.

"You never mentioned a thing," Julia breathed.

Ella shrugged. "Like I said. I never felt like I could rely on anyone except Will. And now?" Tears formed in her eyes and began to streak down Ella's crumpled face. This was it— the wave of sorrow that she'd pushed aside for months.

Alana and Julia hustled around the snack table and wrapped Ella in a hug. Ella shook in their arms, her eyes closed. *Was it better to be held like this? Did it actually help?* She wasn't sure. But in these moments, with the warmth of her sisters' arms around her, she felt protected in a way she hadn't since Will had left. That was something.

"And Danny. He..." Ella felt the words bubbling to the surface. The worry she had for her son felt suddenly too heavy to carry alone.

"What happened?" Alana's eyes shimmered.

Again, Julia and Alana lifted up from Ella. Ella felt like a faucet that couldn't be turned off. Everything burst out from her at once.

"He was taken to the hospital for alcohol poisoning two weeks ago," Ella whispered, terrified at the story all over again. "Laura and I met Will in the emergency room. He was so, so angry. I had said that I would take care of our children. I was so sure that I could!"

"Oh my gosh." All the blood drained from Julia's face.

"But honey, that's not your fault," Alana pointed out. "Teenagers do insane things. Don't you remember my story? Jeremy lost his scholarship because of that stupid accident after the beach party. He had to relearn how to walk."

"Charlie and I drank in high school," Julia added. "It wasn't uncommon. We just had to experiment with our boundaries."

Ella shook her head violently. "I'm sorry. I'm sorry. You just can't understand." She swallowed the lump in her throat.

"Help us understand," Julia begged.

Ella blinked back tears. "The city is not a kind place. Children are tempted with drugs and alcohol in a much different way. Because we're not bringing in money with ticket sales and new albums anymore, I had to take two jobs to make ends meet. I'm not home as much as I should be. I can't monitor Danny's whereabouts. And I'm so terrified that this is going to happen again! What if he accidentally kills himself just because he doesn't know where his boundaries are?"

Ella gasped with panic and smacked her hand over her mouth.

51

Again, Alana and Julia bent down to hug her, this time with more force. Ella hadn't even thought that before, let alone said it. Yet here it was, the truth: she was terrified that Danny would die.

After a long while, Julia released from the hug and dabbed the sleeve of her expensive-looking gown across her cheeks. She eyed the snack table and shivered, clearly at a loss for what to say. "We have to make a plan for how to get you through this."

"There's no plan," Ella whispered. "I'm just going back to Brooklyn. I'm going to make things work."

Julia sighed. "I don't know. I just don't know." Her eyes turned from Alana to Ella and back again. "I think we should change into our pajamas and have a little food. There's so much of it left. And I know I haven't bothered to eat all day long."

"I'm starving," Alana admitted.

Food was the furthest thing from Ella's mind. She wrapped her hands around her elbows and stared at the floor.

"Come on, Ella," Julia breathed. She tugged at Ella's hand like a child.

But before Ella could find the strength to stand, a familiar voice became like music in the beautiful library. "Ella, darling."

The three Copperfield daughters turned to find their mother, Greta, easing through the orange light of the room. Greta had changed into her robe and removed much of her makeup, yet still, she looked regal, like a queen. When she grew closer, her eyes shimmered with tears.

"Ella, I don't know how to tell you this." Greta dropped into the chair beside Ella and gripped her hands.

Ella's heart spun with anxiety. Had her mother heard what she'd said?

"I know I wasn't there for you when you were a teenager," Greta began.

"Mom..." Ella wanted to beg her mother not to go there. Her heart and mind couldn't handle it.

"Honey, please. Let me speak." Greta swallowed. "Back when you were a teenager, I was so lost. I had no concept of anything. I self-medicated. I wasted time. I hardly ate. How stupid I was! How I let you down! I don't know if I'll ever forgive myself. How could I?"

Ella's lips parted with shock. This was a conversation she had never imagined she would have.

"I'm so sorry to have eavesdropped," Greta continued. "I heard what you said about Will, about Danny, about all of it. You must feel very alone and very frightened right now."

Ella wanted to protest, but she couldn't. It was too true. She was so grateful to hear someone else say it.

"Won't you let me help you, Ella?" Greta whispered. "You must be the most stubborn woman in the world, if only because you've had to be. Let the Copperfield women hold you up, just for a little while. There is no reason that you should have to do this alone. Not this time around."

Chapter Seven

The freshman dorm at Columbia University swarmed with fresh-faced eighteen-year-olds, hungry to carve out a space in the world for themselves and their future. Ella waddled back behind the masses with an overstuffed duffel over one shoulder, tugging a suitcase behind her. Laura had another duffel while Alana and Julia struggled forward with boxes of lamps, sheets, toiletries, and other essentials. Somewhere behind them, Danny sulked with his hands in his pockets, refusing to help. Just last night, Ella had broken the news to him that they would return to New York City for one day and one day only— to drop Laura off at college and pack up their things at the Brooklyn apartment. They would be moving to Nantucket for the time being.

Ella knew it was a lot to take in. But she felt she didn't have a choice. What her sisters and her mother had said was the truth. She couldn't live her life alone any longer.

"It's quite different from Rachel's campus," Julia said to Laura. "But you're such a city girl. I guess you wouldn't want something like a big college campus."

Laura laughed nervously and tugged at her hair. "Totally. I couldn't imagine leaving the city."

Having heard, somewhere behind Ella, Danny groaned audibly. Laura turned and locked eyes with her mother, realizing what she'd done.

Ella understood Danny's broken heart. Since the age of eighteen, Ella had counted herself a New Yorker, through and through. Now, she wasn't sure what she was. A washed-up mother of two? A washed-up musician? A woman who'd never married or done anything correctly? Perhaps moving Danny to Nantucket was the first responsible thing she'd ever done.

Laura led Alana, Ella, Julia, and Danny to her floor of the Columbia University Houses, where she would share a room with a girl from Indiana. When they reached Laura's room, the bunkbed remained empty.

"You can grab the bottom bunk!" Ella whispered excitedly.

Laura laughed and dropped her duffel directly on the mattress, which looked pretty clean despite its life as a university dorm room mattress. She then surveyed the room, which was quite small with cinderblock walls and a small window that overlooked the street.

"I guess this is what they call life experience," Laura joked. She then stepped toward Danny and pounded her fist against his upper arm. "What do you think, Bro?"

Danny's cheeks looked sallow. He shifted his weight uncomfortably and eyed every nook and cranny of the little room. "If you and your roommate hate each other, it's going to be a miserable year."

"That's the spirit!" Laura joked, her fists in the air.

"Let's get you unpacked," Ella said, her voice strained. She dropped the duffel on the ground and unzipped it to begin removing sweaters, jeans, and sweatshirts, all of which they'd picked up that morning from the apartment she'd raised her children in. She felt like a boat without a shore.

Everyone else set to work, save for Danny, who sat on the top bunk bed, stared at his phone, and swung his feet through the air. Ella wanted to ask him when he was going to "lose the attitude," but she decided now wasn't the time. Besides, her heart was dark and shadowed by the weight of this day. This was the day her little family would separate even more. How many thousands of nights had she said "good night" to her daughter? How many thousands of nights had she known precisely where Laura was, all tucked safely in bed?

Bit by bit, the little dorm room filled out into a space that was at least half-liveable. Laura placed her newly purchased second-hand laptop on the desk in the corner to claim it as her own. Ella demanded that they take several photographs: one of Ella and Laura, one of Laura and Danny, and a selfie of Julia, Alana, Ella, Danny, and Laura, wherein Danny frowned.

A few minutes before it was time to leave, Will called Laura. Laura answered it with a frantic and high-pitched, "Hi!" She then hurried to the window to peer out as a way to separate her conversation with her father from her mother. "Yeah, we just moved in. It didn't take that long. But Aunt Julia and Aunt Alana helped."

Ella's cheeks were warm with embarrassment. When she lifted her eyes toward her sisters, both gave her horrifically "empathetic" expressions.

"It's really small," Laura continued with a laugh. "My roommate and I will be living on top of each other. Ha, yeah. I hope she likes good music, too."

Julia squeezed Ella's elbow and whispered, "Want to wait in the hallway?"

Ella shrugged lightly, grabbed her purse, and stepped out after Julia. Danny and Alana followed suit, just as Laura burst into another round of laughter at something her father said.

"I'm glad he called," Ella tried.

"He should have been here," Julia interjected.

Danny puffed out his cheeks, clearly just as embarrassed as Ella felt.

"It's really okay." Ella met Alana's, then Julia's gaze. "We're enough."

Ella's heart remained cracked open and bleeding with love for Will. She wasn't sure that feeling would ever go away. She didn't have to translate that to anyone, though. That could remain lodged deep inside. Perhaps inevitably, it would wither and die.

After another minute more, Laura whisked back into the hallway to give everyone a hug. Her eyes were tinged with red, but her smile was electric and optimistic— the stuff of eighteen-year-olds and big dreams. Ella closed her eyes and allowed a few tears to fall as she hugged her daughter close.

"You take care of yourself," she told Laura simply. "I love you to pieces. You know that?"

Laura nodded. Her chin wiggled threateningly, as though she was about to burst into tears. Ella then stepped back, flung up her hands, and said, "Call me if you need anything at all. I can be here in just a few hours. All right?"

Afterward, Ella, Danny, Alana, and Julia piled back into Julia's SUV and returned to Manhattan traffic, which chugged them slowly southeast toward Brooklyn. En route to the apartment where Ella and Will had raised their children and slowly bickered themselves into a separation, Ella received an email from a family man who'd agreed to sublease Ella's apartment. The arrangement went like this: Ella and Danny would pack up their things. Any and all items they wanted to keep but not bring with them to Nantucket would go into storage. The furniture would remain for the subleaser and his family as it was nearly September, and Ella, Danny, Laura, and Will's leftover things needed to be out stat.

"At least the rent is taken care of," Julia said from the driver's seat after Ella explained the terms.

"And you finally called both bosses and quit your jobs, right?" Alana asked.

This had been a relief. Ella's work in food and retail hadn't been thrilling in the slightest. Mostly, her co-workers had been twenty-somethings with dreams to build music, art, or writing careers. To them, Ella's music career was respected, yet still very much over. Each and every day, Ella had felt their waves of pity for her. She'd resented them yet ached with jealousy for them.

Now, she would never have to see them again.

Back at the apartment, Ella gave out tasks. Alana was in charge of cleaning and organizing the kitchen. "The subleaser will use all the plates, cutlery, and kitchen gadgets. Kitchen staples, such as flour, sugar, and oatmeal, can all stay. Just make sure that everything is spick and span, that there is nothing perishable in the fridge, and that there are no personal items in any random drawer," Ella instructed. Alana took over the music room and study while Danny set out to pack up his life into a couple of suitcases.

Ella took over the bedroom she'd shared with Will. When she'd asked him to leave in May, he'd packed up no more than two suitcases and fled to a buddy's place. This meant that the majority of his clothing and odd gadgets remained. Some of his guitars still hung on the wall, and his wide collection of science fiction, literary fiction, and horror novels spread out across the bedroom bookshelves. For more than three months, Ella had lived amongst his things as though pretending that he was on his way home.

They'd brought boxes for the packing. Bit by bit, Ella piled Will's things into boxes and then taped them up. She marked each with a W, feeling as though she was physically "closing" that chapter of her life. When she finished with Will's things, she started on her own, grateful that she'd never been particularly materialistic.

At five that evening, Julia, Alana, Ella, and Danny carried boxes and suitcases into the small storage unit Ella had rented further east in Long Island. After that, they returned to the apartment for a final inspection before they loaded up the rest of Ella and Danny's things and fled the city. They'd decided to drive straight on through the night to get out of the chaos of partying city revelers and expensive restaurants and miles and miles of city blocks that contained too many memories to name. They would stay at a hotel in Hyannis, Massachusetts, and then take the first ferry back to Nantucket the following morning.

Throughout the drive, Danny's mood was ominous. Ella hadn't heard him say a single word in hours. As she sat beside him in the backseat of the SUV, she frequently fought the urge to reach over, grab his hand, and tell him everything was going to be all right. In truth, she had no idea if anything was going to be all right. It was better not to lie.

Julia parked the SUV at the Hyannis Plaza Hotel at ten-thirty that night. The four of them entered the air-conditioned foyer like zombies. Julia, who had the majority of the money just then after the influx of cash from her publishing company, stepped up to the counter and asked for four separate rooms. Ella's heart burst at the show of love and support.

That night, alone in the sterile hotel room, Ella lay face-down and tried to drum up the strength to go to the bathroom and wash her face. Her first thought: *"What's the point?"* was a terrifying one, as it was probably the same question Greta had asked herself during those years that she'd neglected both her and Ella's life. Ella didn't want to be like that.

Suddenly, there was a knock at the door. Ella willed whoever it was to go away; she wasn't in the mood. But another knock, then a "Ella, are you still up?" forced her to hobble toward the door. There, on the other side of the doorframe, stood her gorgeous sisters. Neither wore makeup. Julia carried a bottle of wine, while Alana had three glasses.

"Up for a nightcap?" Alana asked.

Both of their eyes said the same thing: *We know you're miserable. We don't want you to be miserable alone.*

"All right. But just one," Ella insisted as she stepped back, her eyes filling with tears.

The three of them sat cross-legged on the stiff bed with their glasses of wine. From her phone, Alana played music that she'd loved in the nineties, the self-titled album from Shania Twain.

"Oh my gosh. I hated when you played this!" Ella cried, surprised at how hilarious this story was to her now.

Alana danced on the mattress so that it bobbed around beneath her. "You were so pretentious about music, Ella. You never knew how to have fun with it."

"Ha!" Ella dropped her head back, remembering similar conversations that she and Alana had had back in the old days. Things had been so simple back then. It had been "before" so many things had gone wrong.

"Ella may have been pretentious about music, but look how well that worked out for her," Julia said. "Neither of us became professional musicians."

"Sure, sure. But did you ever have fun with music, Ella?" Alana teased. "Real fun?"

Ella's shoulders dropped forward. Her heart felt hollowed out. "For the past thirty years, all I've done is music. It definitely wasn't always fun. But it was like eating or getting enough sleep or drinking enough water. It was what I had to do to survive."

Alana and Julia nodded knowingly. After a long pause, Julia insisted, "Just because you aren't making music with Will..."

"I know. I'll find a way to make music for myself again,"

Ella breathed as her eyes watched the swirling wine in her glass. "But right now, as I pick up the pieces of my broken life, I don't feel even a glimmer of creativity. I feel washed up and tired. And that's the scariest feeling of all, you know? Because I worry that I won't be able to find the music within myself again."

Both Julia and Alana's eyes were consoling, even if Ella felt they couldn't fully understand.

But before Ella or Julia figured out quite what to say to fill the silence, Alana switched the song to Shania's 1995 hit, "Whose Bed Have Your Boots Been Under?" Suddenly, overwhelmed with a mix of emotion and vitality, Ella, Julia, and Alana sang along to the lyrics, dancing gently as Shania swung her southern voice through the playful yet heartbreaking song.

"Ella! You know all the lyrics!" Alana howled.

"Yeah! Because you literally played it one thousand times in the year 1995!" Ella cried.

Alana and Julia tossed their heads back, shaking with laughter. Ella couldn't help but feel, for the briefest of moments, that perhaps everything would be all right. And maybe Alana was right in that sometimes, music didn't have to be so serious. Sometimes, it was all about opening yourself up to the varied experience of being alive.

Chapter Eight

On the morning of Danny's first day of senior year at Nantucket High, Ella's jitters led her to the kitchen table by five-thirty. She sat with a glass of water and a cracker and stared at the waves as they rolled onto the beach, gradually morphing from blacks to soft grays to blues as the light shimmered into the brand-new day. Since they'd packed their bags and "officially" moved into The Copperfield House, Danny had hardly glanced her way. He would make her pay for this decision in the classic "teenage" style: ignoring her. It was the last nail in the coffin of her broken heart.

Ella had decided she would wake Danny up by seven for the eight o'clock start time. Back in Brooklyn, Danny had always been the last to wake up, usually dragging his feet until the very last second, at which point he sprinted out the door like an Olympian. When Ella and Will had asked Laura, "Why is it so easy for you and so hard for him?" Laura had simply said, "I think boys' brains take longer to develop."

This had been a "good" day in Will and Ella's relationship. After Laura's comment, she'd whisked out the door and left

Ella and Will to laugh at Laura's "shade," which was another word that their children had taught them. "Laura just basically said 'girls rule and boys drool,'" Ella had said to Will. "What about that?" To this, Will had said, "I don't have enough brain power to handle both you and a teenage girl. I'm going back to bed."

Ella poured coffee grounds into a filter, added water, and watched as the black liquid strung into the glass pot. Immediately, the soul-warming smell of morning coffee filled the kitchen. Upstairs, footfalls came across the hallway. It was difficult to tell who they belonged to, especially given that there were now six people living in The Copperfield House. Six! That was the original number back in the old days. Outside, a bird squawked with foreboding, as though the first day of school was cause for him to lean into the coming autumn.

"Hey, Mom." Danny appeared in the doorway of the kitchen. He wore a flannel button-down and a pair of nice jeans. He'd showered and wore a hint of cologne. The kind Will had picked out for Danny last Christmas.

The clock on the wall still read six-forty-seven in the morning.

"Danny!" Ella sounded too excited. This was the first time Danny had decided to treat her like a person in many days. "You look really good."

Danny palmed the back of his neck and sat at the kitchen table. The coffee maker continued to gurgle. "I have a meeting with my advisor this morning at seven-thirty," he explained.

In all the chaos of her mind, Ella had forgotten that email several days back, explaining the process of Danny's first day of school. That morning, he would meet with an advisor and select the classes that he felt best aligned with his previous three years of high school and set him up well for college. As far as Ella knew, Danny didn't know what he wanted to do in college— but that was pretty standard amongst seventeen-year-olds. Right?

"Do you have an idea of how you want this year to go?" Ella asked timidly, continuing to stare at the coffee.

"Not really. I mean, I wasn't that bad at Algebra and Geometry. Biology and Chemistry were fun. Maybe I want to go in that direction?" Danny sounded confident and open to anything. Perhaps he'd come to the conclusion that he couldn't very well run off to Brooklyn on his own. The rent was too expensive.

Ella smiled and finally turned her eyes toward her son.

"What?" Danny demanded.

"I don't know. You're just so different from your dad and I."

"Grandpa says that he has scientists on his side of the family," Danny explained.

Ella's eyes widened with surprise. Had Danny spent more time with Bernard beyond that first night of his book release? "Your grandfather is an insanely intelligent person," Ella said instead of asking.

"That's obvious," Danny said, not unkindly.

What had they talked about? Ella burned to know. The coffee pot finished its brewing, and she poured them two mugs of coffee and sat across the table. After Danny took his first sip, he said, "And I've been reading Grandpa's book. The one he wrote in prison."

"Oh. And what do you think of it?" Ella had to admit that the idea had hardly crossed her mind. Julia and Alana had pored over the manuscript countless times for "clues" on the hunt for anything that Bernard's unconscious mind had revealed in the text. Perhaps more and more, Julia was coming around to the fact that it was a work of fiction. Ella thought that was probably healthy.

"His prose is fantastic," Danny said, using a word Ella had never heard him use. "But more than that, I can feel the insane pain he had while he was in prison. The main character talks about sending letters to his wife and not receiving an answer. I mean, that's so devastating. Don't you think? Especially when you think about the fact that he didn't commit the crime."

Ella dropped her gaze to the table, remembering all the letters that had come that she hadn't given to Greta. At the time, she'd needed to protect Greta from tremendous pain. She hadn't considered the pain that had caused Bernard. Back then, he'd been her enemy, the man who'd destroyed her family and left her all alone.

"Are you really sure that he didn't do it?" Ella asked, her voice breathless.

"Aunt Julia says that you three are working tirelessly to prove that it was Marcia Conrad," Danny said. "And if you look at the dates, it adds up. Marcia began her film career directly after she left the Vineyard. Not only that, she directed her own film! Where did she get the capital to finance that?"

"Danny, I don't think we know anything about this Marcia person. Certainly not enough to pin this against her."

"But Alana showed me these emails," Danny continued. "Yes, the text reads a lot like Grandpa's writing. But then again, how do you explain the same exact prose in Marcia's book many years later?"

"I'm sure that happens more than we think," Ella interjected. "Sometimes, I would think that I had written the most incredibly inventive new song, only for someone to say, 'Oh, that's already been done.'"

Danny furrowed his brow, annoyed. Ella bit her tongue. Obviously, if her son wanted to believe in Bernard's innocence, she had to let him. Besides, it seemed his passion behind it had given him a purpose on Nantucket Island.

"But you're right," Ella heard herself say. "There are many questions surrounding what happened with my father and my family all those years ago. If you find any answers, I hope you'll tell your aunts. Or me, I guess."

Danny's eyes brightened slightly. "It's like a detective mystery."

"Something like that."

Ella padded around the kitchen to make her son some eggs and toast. Throughout, Danny chatted evenly about a podcast he'd just listened to about the state of the music industry. Hint: it didn't look good for future indie projects.

As Danny sliced through his eggs and ate, Ella said softly, "I can't believe this is your last 'first day' of school before you run off to college."

What she wanted to say was this: *I'm so glad you made it to your last 'first day' of school and didn't die in that hospital bed.* But she held that in.

Danny rolled his eyes in that classic teenager way. "Yeah, yeah. You're legally supposed to say that because you're my mom."

The walk to Nantucket High School was about a mile. Ella knew the route well. Danny insisted that he didn't want his mother to walk him to school on his first day. Alana, who appeared on the staircase landing with sleep in her eyes, agreed.

"He's seventeen. He has to make an appearance," she scolded Ella.

Ella remembered just how into her appearance Alana had been back in high school, but she kept that to herself. That was a story from another time. Besides, "appearances" were very much important in high school. Ella wasn't so out of touch to remember that.

"I love you!" Ella called from the porch with her hands wrapped around the railing.

Danny waved a sturdy hand back. As he grew smaller and smaller on his walk down the road, he became more and more like his father back in those days— the man who'd changed her life forever. Laura forced her eyes away and realized that Alana remained on the porch with her, bleary-eyed from sleep. Alana placed a hand on Ella's shoulder and said, "I think today calls for a celebration. Don't you?"

Ella groaned. "I don't know if there's anything to celebrate."

"Come on. You just got your youngest off for his last 'first day.' If that's not cause for celebration, I don't know what is."

Alana announced the plan to Julia, who said she needed an hour longer to edit a manuscript and then she could join. One after another, the Copperfield Sisters showered, changed into cute, autumnal outfits, and met in the foyer. They'd asked their mother to join, but Greta had shooed them out, saying, "Enjoy yourselves, you three. You can't always have this old bird around."

The Copperfield Sisters had protested, but eventually, Greta had convinced them. Within minutes, they were headed toward the little brunch place in downtown Nantucket, the adorably-named Black-Eyed Susan's. It was the ultimate in comfort food, with Huevos Rancheros, Cheese Grits, Scrambles with heaps of toppings, Sourdough French Toast, and the world's best coffee (or so everyone said). On that Tuesday morning in early September, several parents of school children sat laughing and gossiping, grateful to have gotten their children off to school on time. Several eyes turned toward Alana, Julia, and Ella, and a few hands even waved. This, Ella knew, was a rarity. But with Julia and Alana's good-will in the community, it seemed that Nantucket Island had begun to forgive the Copperfield Family. For better or for worse.

Although the place was bustling, the waitress seated them in a booth near the window. There, Alana and Julia sat next to the window while Ella remained standing to adjust her long-sleeved top. This was the first time since her "official" move back to Nantucket that she'd been out in public like this. Should she be embarrassed? She wasn't sure.

"Why don't you get the scramble, and I'll get the French Toast, and we can share?" Julia negotiated her breakfast with the urgency of a lawyer.

As Ella turned to sit down, a pair of piercing eyes caught hers. The gaze came from the far corner. After a split-second, a woman in her forties leaped into the air, waved her arms wildly, and then screeched, "Ella Copperfield!"

As the woman breezed across the brunch spot to greet Ella, Ella's heart pounded with fear. *Who was this crazy person? Had anyone ever been so excited to see her?*

But before she could fathom who in the world this was, the stranger's arms were around her. Ella laughed with surprise and then coughed because the woman had taken the air out of her.

"Gosh, I'd heard rumors that you were back. I just wasn't sure." The woman stepped back and flashed a smile Ella would have recognized anywhere.

"Oh my gosh. Stephanie?" Ella's smile nearly cracked her face open. It was her drummer from her very first band, the one who'd snuck off the island all those years ago to play in Greenwich Village. She rushed forward and hugged her ex-best-friend again, overwhelmed.

Stephanie cackled knowingly. When Ella stepped back again, Stephanie was blurry from Ella's tears. Ella tried to take in the full image of this woman, whom she hadn't seen even once since Ella had moved to New York to be with Will and start their band. Stephanie was just as gorgeous, with a little bit of comfortable fluff around the waist that suggested she had children. On her fourth finger, two rings glinted— an engagement band and a wedding band. Clearly, she'd been wealthy in happiness.

"Sit with us!" Alana called over Ella.

Stephanie smiled wider and said, "Are those the other Copperfield Sisters? How did I get so lucky?" She sat across from Ella and said, "I have to get back to my other friend pretty soon. But she can be patient for now. Tell me everything. Are you back-back?"

Ella sat next to Julia and across from Stephanie. "I just moved back home, yep. My son started at Nantucket High this morning, and I'm a nervous wreck."

"You're kidding! My daughter is there. She's a freshman."

"Mine's a senior," Ella affirmed.

"Wow." Stephanie's eyes sparkled. "Who would have thought that our kids would eventually go to school together?"

"It's insanity."

Alana and Julia gave Stephanie brief updates. Throughout, Ella wanted to protest and remind all three of them that Alana and Julia had never really known Stephanie, as they'd hardly been around when their band had really "gotten good." This was petty, though. She knew that.

"And what are you up to these days?" Ella asked, praying that Stephanie wouldn't ask about Will.

"Oh, gosh. I've just been put in charge of organizing the Nantucket Jubilee." Stephanie scrunched her nose nervously, although she was clearly pleased.

Ella shook her head. "What's that?"

"Oh. Let me put on my marketing voice for you," Stephanie joked as she adjusted her posture. "In the year 1820, a whaling ship called The Heart of Nantucket left Nantucket Harbor on a planned one-year whaling quest. That ship did not return the following year and was officially marked as 'lost.' Nantucket families mourned their fathers, brothers, and sons. Until one day in October, two years after its departure, The Heart of Nantucket returned to Nantucket Harbor with all of its men onboard."

69

"Whoop!" Julia clapped her hands. "I forgot about that story."

"It's a good one," Alana confirmed.

"So, it's the two-hundred-year anniversary?" Ella asked.

"That's right," Stephanie replied. "And we're doing it up big. Concerts. Food trucks. Art shows. Even a film festival."

"Wow. A Nantucket Film Festival?" Ella breathed.

Stephanie's eyes bugged out. "I'm literally exhausted. It's been too much to handle. Oh, but we're still on the hunt for musical acts. Do you have any interest in playing for one of the slots?"

Ella's throat tightened. "I don't really have a music project right now."

This, to Ella, sounded like the worst reality in the world. Stephanie took it in stride, as though she'd expected that, anyway. Probably, she knew far more about Ella than Ella knew about her, which gave Stephanie the power.

"That's just fine. Tell you the truth, I haven't touched my drumsticks since you left the island," Stephanie said.

"Oh no!" Ella cried.

"That's fine with me. It was more of a teenage angst thing for me, anyway." Stephanie didn't miss a beat. "But you know, I could really use someone part-time to help with the Nantucket Jubilee. I know you just got back. Maybe you're looking for work?"

Ella's lips parted with surprise. The concept of a "job" had been heavy on her mind, especially because tourist season was preparing to close.

"Are you kidding me?" Ella said, sounding more and more like a teenage girl.

"I'd love your help," Stephanie said. "Here, why don't you put your number in my phone? I can text you with details."

Ella's fingers quivered as she typed out her number. She then passed over the phone and waved a final time to

70

Stephanie, who said, "I still can't believe you're back, Ella. We've missed you around here, you know."

Ella's heart swelled with the memories of those long-ago days when all she'd had was Stephanie and Brenda. Her gaze was again blurry with tears. When the waitress finally returned to take their order, Ella stuttered over the words and finally said, "I'll have what she's having," about whatever Julia had ordered, which made Julia and Alana howl with laughter. Ella had to admit— everything felt especially funny, especially sad, and especially alive just then. She joined along, too.

Chapter Nine

D anny arrived home from his last "first day" of school at three-fifteen. Ella was upstairs in her childhood bedroom, doodling on a guitar, when she heard the door shriek open to announce him. She placed the guitar on the bed and hustled to the staircase to greet him, only to find that Bernard, Greta, Alana, and Julia had all beaten her to the punch. Bernard, whom she hadn't seen since his book release party, seemed almost dressed up in a pair of slacks and a button-down. Even his beard was trimmed and styled with oil.

"How was your first day at school, my boy?" Bernard asked as he clapped Danny on the back.

Ella tip-toed down the staircase, locking eyes with Julia, who looked just as surprised as Ella felt. Bernard had made an appearance to greet Danny after his first day. He'd decided that Danny was enough of a reason to leave his study! *Did that make the rest of them chopped liver? Maybe.* But right then, with Danny's smile playing out across his face as Bernard recited an old quote from Marcel Proust, Ella didn't care what had brought her family together. She was just grateful that her father made an effort.

"How was your first day, honey?" Ella asked when Bernard paused for air.

Danny turned and offered his mother one of his fake smiles. Ella would have recognized it anywhere. Clearly, the first day had been difficult, a series of sights, people, and hierarchies that hadn't existed back in Brooklyn. Teenagers could be cruel.

"It was all right," Danny tried. "I got my classes scheduled."

"That's right!" Bernard spoke with more joy than Ella had seen in over twenty-five years. "Why don't you sit down with me and outline your schedule?"

"That's a great idea," Greta said. "It gives me time to get started on dinner."

Ella, Alana, and Julia exchanged glances. What had gotten into their parents?

Greta beckoned for her daughters to follow her into the kitchen, where a wide array of vegetables gleamed on the countertop and a pot of water already boiled. She announced, "I want Danny to feel at home here. The first day in a new school is no easy feat. To ease him into it, I figured it was time to show him my cooking chops. What do you think?"

Ella's mouth already watered with a thousand memories of Greta's cooking. Alana tugged her luscious hair into a ponytail while Julia headed to the sink to wash the vegetables. Already out on the back porch that overlooked the water, Bernard and Danny were deep in conversation about Danny's math and science interests and the "impossibly beautiful world around them."

It was obvious that when Bernard Copperfield spoke about this "impossibly beautiful world," he also spoke about the twenty-five years that he hadn't been allowed to live in that world. He was very aware of the time he'd lost.

Over the next three hours, Greta, Alana, Julia, and Ella worked diligently to craft an elaborate French meal: chicken à l'orange. Throughout, they alternated between easy chatting, island gossip, and silence so that they could hear the intelligent conversation between Bernard and his grandson.

Ella allowed herself to imagine what this night might have looked like had they stayed in Brooklyn. Probably, she would have had to stay at work till ten-thirty at night. During that time, there was no telling where Danny would have been or what he would have done.

It was better like this. They were safe. They were with family.

At six-thirty, they sat down together as a family, just as they had countless times throughout Ella's childhood. Bernard blessed the meal, he blessed their family, and he thanked Greta for the remarkable gift of cooking she shared. Greta's eyes grew heavy with tears, but she didn't say anything at all.

After the meal, the shadows beneath Bernard's eyes grew heavy. It was clear that he'd overdone it in the social world. Ella stepped toward him to collect his plate and said, "Thank you for celebrating my son's first day."

To this, Bernard grabbed her wrist and said, "Your son is someone very special. I can't tell you how grateful I am to know him."

The words were so precise and so heavy with emotion that they nearly brought Ella to her knees. Before she burst into tears, she hustled herself back to the kitchen, put the plates in the dishwasher, and nearly hyperventilated over the sink. Sometimes, beautiful emotions hurt just as much as sorrowful ones.

* * *

Around eight-thirty that night, Ella joined Alana and Julia in the upstairs study, where Julia read through a potential manuscript for the publishing house, and Alana continued to pore over the court documents for Bernard's case. Ella wanted to roll her eyes at Alana's continued drive to read through every line of the case, but she held herself back. Just as ever, it was difficult to align the crimes Bernard had done with the man she'd just spent the evening with. Gosh, he was just so lovely. Her heart brimmed with love for him.

"I don't know how to tell them that fantasy doesn't sell!" Julia muttered to her manuscript. "This is incredible writing. I just can't take chances like I used to."

Alana blinked up to smile at Ella. "Ignore her. She's been talking to her manuscripts all night."

Ella giggled and sat on the other side of the long table. There, she pulled out the folder of important invoices and bank files regarding the income for her and Will's band over the previous two years. Ella wanted to get a sense of how much money she and Will pulled in for things like merchandise, their inclusion on film soundtracks, and any online streams. Probably, it wasn't that much.

But if she planned to build a life on her own, she had to face the facts. She had to know what was hers and what was his.

Gosh, there were so many numbers. It was difficult for Ella to understand how much of the money they'd been paid went directly to Ella and Will and how much of it went to their agent. Will had always handled that side of things. *Was that wrong?* Probably, she should have sat with him and learned the logistics of the business. She should have gone beyond what she loved to do, which was craft beautiful lyrics and write songs with Will at her side.

"It's wild to me that the music that Will and I wrote twenty years ago is still making the rounds in TV shows and films,"

Ella muttered to her sisters, who glanced up to acknowledge her.

"That's crazy," Alana confirmed.

"Oh, but those first few albums you did were so awesome!" Julia cried, before adding, "And all the others, of course."

"Ha." Ella rolled her eyes. "But the first few ones are nostalgic for people. I get that. I guess that's why they sell so much better."

In truth, those early songs brought in the majority of her yearly wage, even alongside the two jobs she had worked in Brooklyn. The songs were pieces of her heart at this stage of her life. It felt strange that they were also hot commodities.

Throughout this organizational process, Ella used her phone to Google the films and production houses that had purchased the music. It was mostly out of curiosity, as she hadn't paid much attention to films in the past few years. Maybe she would see some of these movies in the theater? Why the heck not? She could take herself on a movie date, all by herself. Since she'd met him, Ella hadn't managed to do anything without Will. Perhaps this would be an expedition into the unknown.

Some of the film production companies were well-known, such as Castle Rock Entertainment, CBS Films, Columbia Pictures, and DreamWorks Animation. Others were lesser known, which intrigued Ella all the more. Who were these people who loved her and Will's music? How did her music fit into the films' stories?

About an hour into her search, Ella discovered a film studio called "Femme Fatale Studios." After a swift search, she found herself staring into the beautiful blue eyes of a very familiar face.

And a split-second later, Ella's tongue went completely dry.

"What the heck?" Ella barely squeaked it out.

Both Alana and Julia lifted their heads with surprise.

"Are you okay, Ella?" Julia leaped from her chair and hustled over to Ella, where she peered down at the image on the screen. "Oh my God. What is Marcia Conrad doing on your phone?"

"Are you kidding me?" Alana hustled over and peered over Ella's opposite shoulder. "Look at that evil face."

Ella shook her head, absolutely aghast. "I was just looking up the various film studios who've purchased the rights to Will and I's music."

"And Marcia came up?" Alana's eyes were wide and panicked.

Ella nodded. "She owns this Femme Fatale Studios. Apparently, they bought the rights to one of our songs as recently as this spring. April, actually."

"The month Dad got out of prison!" Julia exclaimed.

Ella didn't want to jump to any conclusions. "I'm sure it's just a coincidence."

"Come on," Alana scoffed. She then tipped her weight onto the tabletop and tied her hair into a messy bun. "Don't you remember how Marcia bought that painting that Asher made of me?"

Ella did remember that. It was a particularly heinous detail of a particularly heinous portion of Alana's life.

"I mean, how do you explain that?" Alana demanded fiercely.

Ella shrugged. "I don't know."

"I know how," Alana blared. "The woman made a mockery of our family twenty-five years ago. I'm guessing that it was the greatest pleasure of her life. Then, she used that money to start this very production company..." Alana stabbed her finger directly next to Ella's phone. "And she's collecting the rest of our projects like a hunter collecting the heads of animals."

"Alana, that's insane," Ella tried. She turned to catch Julia's eyes, hoping for a voice of reason.

But Julia just shook her head. "This woman is a master manipulator. I wouldn't put anything past her."

"I mean, there were loads of fans of my band," Ella pointed out. "Maybe she just happened to be one? That, or she wasn't even in charge of securing the rights of the music."

Alana and Julia cast one another doubtful looks. Ella saw that she was playing a losing game.

"Maybe you should ask Will about it," Alana tried.

"Not that we think you should reach out to Will if you don't want to," Julia interjected. "I, for one, am much happier without Jackson in my life."

"Oh, gosh. I only deal with Asher through lawyers," Alana confirmed.

"I've been meaning to ask you about that clause in your divorce paperwork," Julia began, a finger outstretched.

In a flash, Julia and Alana returned to one of their favorite topics of conversation: their ongoing divorces. Slowly, they moved back to their seats and exchanged stories about the horrific things their exes had done or said over the years.

This left Ella in a whirlwind. In truth, she and Will hadn't had some kind of volatile breakup. Bit-by-bit, they'd fallen apart.

And she was often left with the question: if they had actually gotten married somewhere along the way, would they have worked harder to stay together? Was their lack of legal binding allowing them to trash what they should have repaired?

It didn't matter. Not now.

Ella returned her paperwork to its files, X-ed out the website for Marcia Conrad's production studios, and said goodnight to her sisters. Perhaps that night, she would find a way to sleep.

Chapter Ten

S everal days later, Ella stepped out of the Nantucket Community Music Center, where she'd met Stephanie and the rest of the Nantucket Jubilee crew to plan the next steps in the elaborate and all-consuming October event. Stephanie burned with beautiful energy as she spoke about the event and "honoring Nantucketers from two hundred years back, without whom we wouldn't be where we are today." It was exhausting yet soul-warming. Ella was grateful she'd found this niche for herself, if only because it allowed the days to pass more swiftly.

Once outside, a September breeze swept through Ella's trench coat and whipped it back. Trees that lined the downtown streets had edged their leaves with reds, yellows, and oranges. Still, across the Nantucket Harbor, sailboats shifted against the docks, and tourists and locals alike embarked out across the Sound, grateful for the shimmering autumnal sun.

In her pocket, Ella's phone began to buzz. She lifted it to discover a strange yet very welcome name: WILL. *When was the last time they'd spoken?* The answer came quickly. It had been the night that Danny had been in the hospital. More than a week ago, Ella had simply texted Will about her decision to move Danny to Nantucket High, which had resulted in a two-hour phone conversation between Danny and Will, most of which Ella hadn't been able to hear. (What she had heard was Danny saying over and over again, "It isn't fair, Dad. It just isn't fair." Incidentally, this was exactly how Ella felt about everything in her life.)

Ella's voice sounded childish. "Hi!"

Will's wasn't much better. "Hello, there."

Silence. Ella's stomach twisted. She was reminded of high school when Will would use a pay phone to call The Copperfield House from New York City. "How is the tour going?"

"Not bad," Will replied. "We're in Portland, Oregon right now."

"Wow. I always loved it there." Ella hated that she immediately went to old memories of herself and Will in Portland. Once, they'd even talked about moving there.

"I know."

Had Will called her because Portland had made him think about the good times?

"Anyway." Ella reached the railing that separated the boardwalk and the water below. "Danny is settling into Nantucket High."

"Yeah. He texted me to say it was 'kind of lame but mostly fine,'" Will joked.

"That sounds like Danny," Ella breathed. After a pause, she added, "I'm sorry that I didn't include you in that decision."

It had been the first childrearing decision she'd ever made by herself.

"It's okay," Will offered. "I was initially angry that you'd left me out, but then I thought about it and understood. Maybe, in hindsight, the city wasn't the best place to raise our family."

"Laura made it out okay," Ella tried.

"Laura would make it anywhere," Will quipped. "She's an anomaly."

Ella laughed, terrified at how good it was to joke around with Will. It was almost as though he stood right beside her, watching the boats. An instinct to tell him how much she loved him swelled over her, but she shoved it away.

They spoke of other things. Will told a story about his gig in Sante Fe, where a naked man had run through the crowd and howled, "The nineties aren't dead!"

"We weren't even a nineties band," Ella pointed out, chuckling.

"I know! But I appreciated his spirit," Will said. "I guess he was probably disappointed that you weren't on stage."

Ella couldn't even begin to approach that statement. She swallowed the lump in her throat and said instead, "I was going over some of the band paperwork the other night."

"Oh, man. Organization is the last thing on my mind right now."

"I remember what touring was like," Ella quipped. "It's a wonder if you manage to eat and sleep enough, let alone everything else."

"Exactly," Will said. "Thank you for going through all that."

"Sure." Ella's heart skipped a beat. "I didn't realize we had so many songs coming out in films and TV shows just this year."

"Yeah. People are really into the nostalgia of our music, I think," Will said. "But it'll be healthy for our bank accounts, right?"

"No doubt about that." Ella pushed herself to ask what she needed to ask. "The thing is, one of the production companies really surprised me."

"Which one?"

"Femme Fatale Studios," Ella said. "It's owned by this woman named—"

"Marcia," Will interrupted her. "Marcia Conrad. Yeah."

"Yeah?" Ella's ears began to ring. Far out at sea, a boat's sails flashed with the severity of the sun. "You know her?"

"Sure!" Will seemed energetic. "Marcia contacted me last year about the song being used in her upcoming film. I checked out her work and was really impressed. She has clearly paved the way for other women in literature and film."

"Right..." Ella's ears continued to scream. *Was this actually happening?* "The thing is..."

"In fact," Will continued, "during our stopover in Los Angeles, Marcia came to the gig and asked to buy me a drink after."

Ella's stomach swirled, threatening to throw up the small cookies she'd eaten at the Nantucket Jubilee planning meeting. "Oh," was all she managed to say.

"Yeah. She's such a smart cookie," Will continued, unprompted. "She said the film's going to premiere in the next month or so. I can't wait to see how she uses our song."

Ella tried to find a way to explain to Will just how strange this was. Number one, Marcia Conrad had been Bernard Copperfield's "mentee" and "potential mistress" there at The Copperfield House. (Just because her sisters and mother no longer believed that didn't mean that Ella didn't.) Number two, Marcia had left the island very soon before the accusations against Bernard Copperfield came to light. Number three, Marcia had purchased the painting of Alana that Alana herself had destroyed.

Number four, not only had Marcia asked for the rights to one of Ella's songs; in fact, she'd actually gone on a date with Will. It was head spinning.

Was it possible that Alana, Julia, and Danny were correct?

Ella had been quiet too long. Will had begun to suspect something.

"Ella, what's up?" His voice was dark.

"Um." How could she explain?

"Ella, come on. Don't you remember that you were the one who asked me to leave?" Will demanded. "You were the one who decided it was over."

"That's not totally fair," Ella whispered.

"Ella, we're both going to have to find ways to move on," Will insisted. "We're going to go on dates with people. We're going to find new ways to love people."

Ella felt outside of her body. *Was Will, the love of her life, really saying this to her? This was a nightmare.*

"I think I have to go," Ella told him. If she didn't, she would burst into tears.

"Ella, please." Will's voice had softened.

"No. It's fine. Really." Ella closed her eyes to allow tears to escape. "I hope you have a good time in Portland. Please, eat a Voodoo Doughnut for me. You know how I've craved them ever since our last trip."

"I will."

Ella hung up the phone, shoved it in her purse, and placed her face in the crook of her elbow as she leaned against the railing. There, she was allowed a brief moment of darkness, even as the autumn sun roared above her. There, she could feel the depths of her sorrow, knowing that Will was out there, open to dates with other women and whatever came next.

We're going to go on dates with people. We're going to find new ways to love people.

It was a nightmare. Illogically, Ella hadn't imagined either of them ever falling in love again. After all, they'd been each other's worlds since eighteen and nineteen. How could anyone else fit into that?

Chapter Eleven

When Danny announced that he had gone out for the Nantucket High School Football Team, Ella nearly dropped her yogurt cup. She gaped at her lanky son, at the fingers that had never managed to piece together many guitar chords, and at the shoulders that seemed built for muscles that he'd just never bothered to grow. Perhaps that was due to city life. Now, he was in the natural world and ready to fill out and become a man.

"Yeah. I'm faster than most guys in gym class," Danny explained as he set his calculus and biology textbooks on the kitchen table. "The gym teacher suggested I swing by football practice to talk to the football coach, who just so happens to be Aunt Alana's boyfriend, Jeremy. He said he wants me to start going to practice starting tomorrow. It's every day, though, which is insane."

"What!" Ella sat at the edge of the kitchen chair and abandoned her yogurt cup. "You're going to wear a football jersey? And the shoulder pads? And the cleats?" It was difficult to picture.

"Yeah. I'm pretty sure that's what they all wear," Danny said, rolling his eyes. "Anyway, that's why I'm a little late."

"Alana!" Ella howled like a dog.

Alana whipped out from the residency side of The Copperfield House, where she was prepping for her actress seminar. She brought a wave of expensive perfume with her. "What's up? Did something happen?"

"Danny is playing on Jeremy's football team," Ella said, awestruck.

Alana's smile burst. "He texted me about it. He couldn't believe how fast Danny could run."

Danny rolled his eyes, even though his face glowed with clear pride. "He told me I have to call him Coach Farley from now on."

"Oh, gosh. Arrogant, much?" Alana was pleased. "I guess we'll see you at the game this Friday?"

"Mom? You in?" Danny asked.

Ella chuckled. "I don't know if I ever went to a Nantucket High School football game, even when I was going to Nantucket High."

"That's because your mom thought she was cooler than everyone," Alana explained sassily.

"It's a little more complicated than that," Ella insisted as Alana and Danny laughed. "But okay. Okay. I'm excited about this. I'll wear a shirt with your name on it, Danny Boy."

"Oh. Please don't," Danny said.

It was a funny thing, grappling with all these Nantucketer ways of life. Ella found herself falling deeper in love with the slower pace, the easy mornings at The Copperfield House, and the delightful banter with everyone who worked on Nantucket Jubilee. Perhaps becoming a "football mom" was just another step on the road to becoming more "Nantucketer." She shoved aside old instincts and told herself to embrace the change.

Just like Will was, all the way across the country.

* * *

That Friday night, a September chill whipped across the island and sent the temperature to fifty-seven degrees. After such a warm and often suffocating summer, the air felt remarkably cold and refreshing. Ella, Alana, and Julia bundled up in sweaters, scarves, and jackets and set out for the Nantucket football field, where they planned to sip warm apple cider and watch Nantucket High play Oak Bluffs High School from Martha's Vineyard. This was one of Nantucket's top rivalries, and it always made for a "great game," or so Nantucketers said. Ella wasn't sure.

Ella fetched them three hot apple ciders and joined Alana and Julia at the top of the stands, which offered the best view of the lush green field. The game would begin in five minutes, and already, the stands were jam-packed with Nantucket and Oak Bluffs fans.

As Ella settled in beside Julia, she couldn't help but notice that many eyes peered up and over at them from all ends of the stands.

"Ignore them," Julia instructed under her breath. "It takes getting used to, but Alana and I are finally getting the hang of it."

Suddenly, Alana burst to her feet and howled, "Go get 'em, Jeremy!" She no longer seemed like the young woman who'd been embarrassed about basically everything. Now, she was willing to be public about her fresh love for Jeremy Farley and embrace what it meant to be a Nantucketer.

How strange, Ella thought. And yet, how beautiful.

A few minutes before the game began, a man with a microphone introduced the teams. "Good evening, ladies and gentlemen. Let me welcome you to the most competitive event of the season: the football match between Oak Bluffs and Nantucket High!"

Ella was surprised to hear herself howl along with the others, caught up in the pomp and circumstance. They were just as loud as any crowd at a concert venue, maybe louder.

"Look! There's Danny!" Ella suddenly cried out, pointing her free finger toward the lanky teenager who palled along with the other football players as though he'd always belonged.

Julia chuckled. "I'm like you. I can always recognize my kids at a distance, even when they're in disguise."

"If you had told me last year that Danny would be the staring running back for Nantucket High School, I would have laughed myself to the psych ward," Ella said, her eyes widening.

"If you'd have told me last year that I would ever go to a football game again— let alone cheer on my boyfriend, the high school football coach? I would have probably sipped my thousand-dollar champagne and called you a fool," Alana said.

"Thousand-dollar champagne?" Alana's previous all-expenses-paid lifestyle with her ex, Asher, still shocked Ella.

Alana raised a shoulder. "It wasn't great. Just really good."

Julia and Ella locked eyes and shared a secret laugh just as the football team lined up on the field to prepare for their very first play.

"I wish I knew one thing about football," Ella breathed nervously.

"You do," Julia pointed out. "Remember, they have to get that ball thingy over that last white line over there."

"It seems a little more complicated than that." Ella laughed nervously as, suddenly, her son sprinted forward, his arms extended. With an ecstatic burst of energy, he nabbed the football out of the sky.

Ella, Julia, and Alana howled with excitement. A few rows in front of them, an older Nantucketer asked his wife, "Who is that new running back?"

"I heard he was related to the Copperfields in some way," his wife whispered back, just loud enough for Ella to hear.

"Well, if he has any of Bernard's talents, let's hope he robs Oak Bluffs of this win," the guy said.

Ella's shoulders dropped. Around her, the crowd quieted as the football players set back up on the field. To Ella, it seemed that the players whispered secrets to one another immediately before the "play." Would Ella ever understand what went on down there? Maybe she was okay, staying in the dark.

About ten minutes into the clock (which equated to about twenty-two minutes of actual time), the other team called a time-out. Ella, Alana, and Julia glanced at one another, then laughed at how serious they all looked.

"I guess we're really taking this seriously," Julia said.

"Who knew that the Copperfields could ever care about sports?" Alana offered.

Ella sipped her cider, which had grown lukewarm. On the field, both teams huddled, discussing the game as though it was war.

"I talked to Will on the phone the other day," Ella said suddenly, surprising herself. It wasn't like her to share the news of her heart.

Both Julia and Alana turned back to face her, their faces marred with shock.

"Did he call?" Julia asked.

"Finally," Alana interjected. "You've only moved his daughter into college and put his son into a safer school. The least he could do was call."

Ella grimaced. "To tell you the truth, it was so good to hear from him. At first."

"Uh oh," Julia moaned.

"It was just like old times. He talked about the tour and even mentioned some memories we shared while making music together. For a little while, I could pretend like we'd never broken up," Ella continued. "And then, I decided to ask him about Marcia Conrad."

Julia and Alana's eyes widened.

"Apparently, she contacted him last year about using the song on her new film." Ella's voice broke. "And the two of them hit it off. Marcia came to their show out in LA recently, and afterward, the two went out together."

Julia and Alana looked stricken. Out on the field, the players had begun to line up again for another round.

"You're telling us that Marcia Conrad went on a date with your husband?" Alana muttered, her voice venomous.

"We never got married," Ella interjected, saying it instinctually.

"That doesn't matter," Alana coughed. "Marcia knows exactly what she did."

Ella now wished she hadn't brought up the Marcia Conrad situation. It felt too heavy to carry just then. Plus, neither Julia nor Alana was invested in the football game any longer. Both clearly wanted to return to the matter at-hand: revenge.

"Let's just talk about it later," Ella whispered, suddenly exhausted.

"It just adds fuel to the fire," Julia said. "She's being so obvious about it."

"We have to take her down." Alana smashed her fist in her opposite palm.

"Yeah. Maybe by then, Will and Marcia will have already gotten married," Ella said ruefully, surprising herself yet again with how eager she was to share her thoughts with her sisters.

Julia touched Ella's shoulder delicately. "Ella, that just won't happen."

Ella's eyes flashed. "Crazier things have happened."

Neither Alana nor Julia knew what to say to that. Out on the field, Oak Bluffs' football team managed to make a field goal, which, as Ella now knew, gave them three points. Nevertheless, Nantucket remained in the lead by ten. Ella crossed her fingers for a Nantucket victory and tried to shove all thoughts of Marcia Conrad from her mind. Marcia couldn't taint this night, too.

* * *

That night after the football game, Bernard and Greta made a fire out on the sand. The orange light licked at the impossibly dark sky and taunted the volatile ocean. As Ella, Danny, Alana, and Julia approached, Bernard waved a sturdy hand in greeting and said, "Danny, I want a play-by-play. Get on over here."

"And we have ingredients for s'mores!" Greta announced brightly.

Greta and Bernard were seated on opposite sides of the fire. Ella wondered who, between them, had decided upon the fire. *Had they spoken as they'd put the firewood together? Was there any romance between them at all? Or did they consider their long-ago marriage someone else's memories?*

As Danny explained the ins-and-outs of the football game to his grandfather, Alana, Julia, Greta, and Ella sat close and watched the fire. Julia reported who they'd seen up at the football stadium, including old friends of Greta's, most of whom Greta hadn't spoken to in decades. Greta reacted kindly and said, "Oh, I've often wondered how they've been. How do they look?"

To this, Julia said simply, "Not as good as you, Mom. But you know that."

Greta cackled good-naturedly. As she slid a marshmallow onto the sharp edge of a stick, she adjusted her face, captivating her daughters. It was clear that she had something to say.

With the marshmallow at the outer edge of the flickering flame, Greta said under her breath, "I was in the study today, girls, and I came across all that silly paperwork from a court case that happened a long, long time ago."

Julia, Alana, and Greta all sent one another worried glances. It was almost as though their mother had caught them doing something illegal as teenagers.

Greta's face was stoic, her eyes catching the light of the fire ominously. Under her breath, she said, "We need to get past this. As a family."

"We're just trying..." Alana began.

But Greta spoke sharply. "Our family has been through enough, Alana. Now that Danny is here and the book has been released, the Copperfields are back on track. Let's not dig any deeper into that mess, all right?"

Unsure of what else to do, Alana, Julia, and Ella nodded their heads, reached for marshmallows of their own, and began to toast them to perfection. All the while, however, Ella's thoughts burned with a desire to take Marcia Conrad down. She'd come for Will, and that was inexcusable. Period.

Chapter Twelve

The Nantucket Jubilee Organizational Meeting ended at one-thirty on a Wednesday in Mid-September. As the other Nantucketers weaved out of the Nantucket Community Musical Center, their Nantucket Jubilee tasks written in their planners and their mouths ready for whatever gossip the afternoon would bring, Stephanie dropped her face into her hands and said, "Oh my gosh, Ella. I'm in over my head."

Ella rubbed her shoulder, just as she'd done back in the old days when Stephanie had said, "I can't drum a second longer! It hurts too much!"

"You're killing it," Ella said now. "The Jubilee is coming together. Plus, we have three more weeks."

"I know!" Stephanie cried. "But when I dismissed the meeting, I realized that I'd completely forgotten to talk about selecting the venues for the films that are coming to the film festival. The film people are set to arrive several days before each viewing to make sure the cinemas are all set up. That means it's like an immediate priority!"

Stephanie dropped her hands from her eyes to show the early signs of a breakdown.

"Okay! Okay. It's okay." Ella was surprised at how optimistic she sounded. "You know what I do when I get this freaked out?"

Stephanie shook her head, wrinkling her brows together in confusion.

"I go and get something to eat," Ella said. "Why don't we take all this work to Black-Eyed Susan's, order some eggs and French toast, and make a to-do list?"

"Are you sure? Don't you have enough on your plate?" Stephanie asked.

Ella did, in fact, have a number of other tasks to complete for the Nantucket Jubilee. That said, she couldn't leave Stephanie in a lurch like this.

"I'm sure," Ella said. "Plus, I'm starving. Don't make me beg you to go."

Fifteen minutes later, Stephanie and Ella sat across from each other at Black-Eyed Susan's, watching through the window as September tourists attempted to cling to what was left of summer. They were wrapped in cardigans, eating ice cream cones, and pretending that winter wouldn't come.

Ella and Stephanie ordered French toast, cheese grits, and the largest cups of coffee the place had. Then, Stephanie began to talk very quickly about Nantucket venues, the "pop-up" cinemas they planned to arrange for, and the multiple directors, writers, and actors they planned to host. It was all a lot, especially for such a small island.

"I told the mayor that we hoped to compete with modern festivals like the Tribeca Film Festival and Venice Film Festival," Stephanie explained. "But I'm beginning to feel that that was naive?"

"No," Ella assured her, although she believed that it had been naive, very much so, especially given what she knew about music festivals in general. "I don't see why we can't make this work."

Stephanie began to make stacks of paperwork across the table, labeling each with a separate post-it note. "This stack includes paperwork we still need to fill out to officially rent out the venues. This stack involves insurance that we still need to secure. This stack is a list of the filmmakers, actors, and writers who plan to come, which hotels we've lined up for them, when and if we've asked them to speak to festival guests. and a list of their demands."

Ella laughed. "Demands?"

Stephanie nodded. "I figured you would understand that. When you were on tour, didn't each venue ask you for your demands? Like, I read that Madonna requested a brand-new toilet seat at every venue."

"Well, Will and I were never Madonna, Beyoncé, or Lady Gaga," Ella pointed out. "We were just an indie band with a moderately big following."

Stephanie looked confused for a moment. "So, you never requested anything insane backstage?"

"Did some of these people send along their demands for the Nantucket Jubilee?" Ella asked, flipping through the stack of papers.

"A few actors and actresses asked for specific brands of water and champagne," Stephanie said.

"That shouldn't be too difficult," Ella said as she read over the small list of prominent actors and actresses, all of whom had been in major motion pictures in the past three years. Two of them had been nominated for Oscars.

"I'm going to start calling these venues," Stephanie said, pointing to the first stack. "Maybe you could go through that stack and book hotel suites for each director, actor, and screenwriter?"

Ella saluted Stephanie and said, "Aye, aye, captain."

Over the next forty minutes, Stephanie and Ella worked diligently. Between phone calls, they nibbled on cheese grits and French toast, sipped their coffee, and gave one another thumbs-ups.

"Good afternoon, this is Nantucket Suites. My name is Rita. How may I help you?" A woman greeted Ella warmly and succinctly.

"Hi!" Ella said. "My name is Ella, and I'd like to book a room for one of the Nantucket Jubilee's celebrity guests."

"How exciting," Rita said. "May I have a name and your dates?"

"The actress is named Isabella Thornberg. She arrives Wednesday, October 5th, and will stay until Monday, October 10th."

"Marvelous. I look forward to her appearance in *Sweet Relief.*"

"Oh!" Ella was surprised that Rita knew the name of the film. Ella herself hadn't yet glanced at the film list. "That's a good title."

"Isn't it? I've heard it's a psychological thriller," Rita said, suddenly becoming chummy. "Although you know, Marca Conrad's films are never what they seem to be on the surface. Sometimes, I watch them two nights in a row, just to see them from different perspectives."

Ella's jaw dropped. Here she was again. Marcia Conrad.

"Oh, sorry. I'm not supposed to get so animated on the phone," Rita said, now dialing back her excitement. "You said Isabella Thornberg from the fifth to the tenth."

"I did." Ella's throat felt terribly tight.

"Is Marcia staying here at the Nantucket Suites as well? I heard a little rumor on a film website that she would be making an appearance."

"Let me check," Ella said, flipping through the rest of the stack of papers frantically until she found Marcia Conrad's file.

There, Marcia's horrific yet beautiful smile blared at her in black and white. Beside Marcia's name read: *No hotel booking required; Ms. Conrad has arranged private accommodations.*

"It looks like Ms. Conrad already has something arranged," Ella said.

"Oh, shoot." On the other end of the line came the sound of Rita's fingers across a keyboard. "I have Isabella all booked for you, though. Can I have an email address so that I can pass along that information?"

Ella worked on autopilot, giving the Nantucket Jubilee official email to Rita. After that, she wished Rita a beautiful day and jumped off the phone. For a full thirty seconds, she stared down at the sinister, smiling face of Marcia Conrad.

Marcia was making it very difficult for Ella not to believe she was up to something.

Stephanie was now off the phone, jotting notes to herself and nibbling at the French toast. "You've been such a big help. I can't even begin to tell you how much better I feel..."

But Ella just shook her head in shock.

Stephanie's eyes jumped back toward Ella's face. She stopped chewing. "Are you all right?"

Ella sensed that all of the blood had dropped from her face. She felt woozy. "Yeah."

Stephanie spotted Marcia Conrad's file directly below Ella. "Do you know who that is?" Stephanie asked brightly.

"Um. I think so?" Ella lied.

"Apparently, she's this top-shot director," Stephanie explained excitedly. "I couldn't believe it when she reached out and said she wanted to premiere her film here at the film festival. Seriously, it's what led me to tell the mayor that we could compete with the Venice Film Festival."

"Ah. I see." Ella felt speechless.

"Anyway, my kids have told me that she's a mega-star," Stephanie continued. "She's premiering this new film called

Sweet Relief and has agreed to do an interview afterward. Oh! I forgot the most important part."

Ella's eyes had fully dried out. "What's that?"

"Apparently, Ms. Conrad has a history on Nantucket," Stephanie continued. "And has a friendship with Gregory Puck."

Gregory Puck was one of the men Bernard had stolen millions from. Back in 1997, Gregory Puck had sat to testify that Bernard, his best friend for decades, was a "thief and a liar." Probably, Stephanie's memory of the Copperfield trial had faded. Back when it had happened, they'd been too young to understand the intricacies of such a trial, anyway.

"Anyway, Gregory Puck has asked to give a speech about Ms. Conrad's efforts in the film industry and the start she got here on the island," Stephanie continued, beaming with optimism. "Can you believe it, Ella? I really think this is going to be an excellent festival. I can feel it in my bones."

Somehow, Ella worked her way through the rest of her stack of paperwork, paid for her half of breakfast, walked Stephanie back to the Nantucket Community Music Center, and returned to The Copperfield House without sobbing with rage. She felt like a trapped animal; all the exits seemed to lead directly to Marcia Conrad's beautiful, successful face.

When Ella returned, she sat on her childhood bed with her guitar in her lap and strummed chords angrily, like a teenager with an attitude problem. Then, she grabbed her computer and searched for Marcia Conrad's website. A CONTACT MARCIA box sat there provocatively, and Ella didn't have the willpower not to type in it.

It was childish, maybe. But at the moment, it felt like the only way.

ELLA: I know what you're doing. Stay away from my family. Or else my sisters and I will find a way to make you pay for what you did.

97

With that, she pressed SEND and dropped back on her bed, completely satisfied. She'd never resorted to these sorts of tactics. Yet now, as she lived a life she didn't fully understand, she watched herself do and think and feel things she never had before. It was a new era.

Chapter Thirteen

Alana and Julia were flabbergasted at the news of Marcia Conrad's involvement in the Nantucket Jubilee. "That snake!" Alana cried, clutching her mug of coffee the next morning. "She's gone too far this time!" Julia agreed. Unfortunately, nobody knew quite what to make of it, nor how to decide what to do next. Ella decided not to tell her sisters that she'd reached out to Marcia herself via Marcia's website. It had been a moment of passion and anger, and it would probably amount to nothing. Probably.

Despite the drama with Marcia and the chaos of the impending Nantucket Jubilee, things on Nantucket had more-or-less settled into themselves. As running back on the Nantucket football team, Danny had already become "somebody to know" amongst the seniors, with girls hanging around him a little too long after the football games and guys asking him over to play video games and shoot hoops. It warmed Ella's heart to see Danny fall so easily in with this less-raucous islander crowd. He still chatted with his Brooklyn pals, she knew, but he no longer seemed to demonize her for her decision to move them out of the city. Perhaps, even at seventeen, he understood why she had had to.

About a week and a half after learning of Marcia Conrad's involvement with the Nantucket Jubilee, Ella returned home from a Jubilee meeting to find Alana, Jeremy, Charlie, and Julia out on the back porch. It was a Thursday, a gorgeous sixty-seven degrees, with tufts of clouds floating against a cerulean sky. Charlie played a Johnny Cash album on his portable speaker and flipped burgers on the grill that sat near the steps that led up to the porch. Jeremy stood with his muscular arms wrapped around Alana's stomach while Julia placed a juicy-looking watermelon at the center of the table.

"I couldn't believe it," Julia said. "There was one more good watermelon at the store, and I grabbed it before anyone else."

"Thatta girl," Alana teased. "You always get what you want."

Ella laughed and sat at the table. A breeze fluttered in off the Nantucket Sound and swept her hair out behind her.

"That kid of yours has really changed our game," Jeremy said to Ella.

"I never thought in a million years that I would be the mother of a jock," Ella joked.

"He's just well-rounded," Julia countered.

"I wish someone could convince me to do a little more exercise," Alana said. "Ever since I got back to this island, I've been overfed and overly lazy."

"Come on, Alana," Ella said. "There's nothing wrong with a little overindulgence."

"Tell that to my jeans!" Alana quipped.

Julia returned to the table with a bottle of sparkling water with lemon. While the girls sipped the fresh and citrusy water, Charlie drank a diet soda, and Jeremy drank Gatorade, as he had football practice in a little while and planned to join the football players in a two-mile run. Out across the beach, a little girl rushed into the wall of wind, tugging a bright pink kite along with her. Sometimes, the island seemed too picturesque.

For a brief and beautiful moment, everything in Ella's life seemed perfect.

Next came a knock at the door. Ella said, "I got it," and carried her glass of water back inside. Julia hollered, "Could you grab the bag of lime tortilla chips on the counter?" "Of course, sis," Ella called back. It would be a blissful afternoon with her sisters and her sisters' boyfriends. Ella would do her best to shove away all thoughts of sorrow about being single again. Being single was often a blessing; at least, that's what so many magazines and books advertised.

Ella opened the front door to find a broad-shouldered and muscular man of five-foot-six dressed in a mail courier's uniform. The man carried a large manila envelope.

"Hello, there!" The courier was chipper, showing a big gap in his teeth.

"Hi!" Ella could find no reason not to be just as friendly.

"Are you Ella Copperfield?" the man asked.

"I am." Ella glanced at the manila envelope, stretched out her hands, and accepted it. She assumed that the envelope had something to do with Will and Ella's band, Danny's new school, Laura's new university, or the Nantucket Jubilee.

"I just need you to sign for this," the courier said.

Ella flourished her signature across the page without a second thought. She then said, "Have a beautiful day!" and turned on her heel to head back inside. She placed the manila envelope on the kitchen table, grabbed the bag of lime tortilla chips, and returned to the back porch. She would deal with the logistics of that later.

"Who was at the door?" Julia held her tortilla chip near her lips.

"It was a mail courier," Ella explained. "Something to do with the band, I'm guessing. Or Danny's school."

"Oh, gosh. You didn't look?" Julia's smile widened. "When I don't open my mail, the anxiety of what I don't know follows me around the rest of the day."

Ella snorted. "I have enough anxiety right now. There's no way I can add to it."

"Famous last words," Charlie said, waving his spatula.

Ella ate a chip slowly and sipped her sparkling water. Charlie lined the burgers across a large white plate while Julia fetched the mustard, ketchup, sliced tomatoes, onions, and lettuce from the fridge. A small seed of dread had been planted in her stomach, but she'd decided to ignore it for now. The manila envelope couldn't bite her, whatever it contained.

"Can I ask a question?" Jeremy's eyes flashed dangerously as he tapped a napkin across his lips and set down his burger.

"Uh oh," Alana joked.

"I'll ask it anyway," Jeremy said. "Your parents. Are they...?"

"What?" Julia asked, playing dumb.

"I mean. Are they together?" Jeremy asked.

Alana hissed, "Quiet down! Dad always keeps his study window open."

"Oh, who cares if he hears?" Jeremy said. "They must know that everyone's curious about it. They're still married, after all."

"As far as I know, Mom sees Dad as often as we do," Julia said. "Which, admittedly, has been more since Danny came around."

"But it hasn't seemed romantic," Ella affirmed.

"That's too bad," Charlie said softly. "They both deserve love in their lives. I hope they find a way to either move on from one another or come back together again." He glanced lovingly toward Julia and took her hand across the table.

This sent Ella into a tailspin. After all, didn't this echo what Will had said recently about "moving on"? Although she still hadn't finished her burger, she stood quickly and nearly toppled her chair to the ground. "Whoops! I'm so clumsy today. I don't know what's going on." Ella tried on a smile and then said, "Does anyone need anything?"

"We're all set," Julia said.

Ella padded back inside, gripped the edge of the kitchen counter, and told herself to get a grip. There in the privacy of the kitchen, she tried to stamp out her anxiety. Outside on the back porch, her sisters and their boyfriends howled with laughter at a joke Ella hadn't heard.

Ella turned back to grab the manila envelope. Maybe Julia was right. It was better to stare whatever this was in the face, deal with it, and move on. That way, it wouldn't nag at her throughout the afternoon and make her even crazier.

Ella used a knife to slice the top of the manila envelope precisely. Then, she removed the small stack of printouts and placed them in front of her.

At the very top of the stack was a black-and-white copy of a birth certificate. Ella turned it so that she could read it.

Commonwealth of Massachusetts
Registry of Vital Records and Statistics
CERTIFICATE OF LIVE BIRTH
Name: Ella Blackwood
Date of Birth: July 12, 1980
Place of Birth: Nantucket Cottage Hospital
Mother: Joni Blackwood

For a long and powerful moment, Ella didn't think of anything at all. She simply read the words and the date of birth and hardly considered that this piece of paper would rock the foundation of her world forever. Then, she leaped from the kitchen chair, bug-eyed.

July 12th, 1980 was her birthday.

Ella was her name.

But who was Joni Blackwood? What on earth did this mean? And why the heck had someone sent this to her, out of the blue, on a random Thursday in September— when she was forty-two years old?

Ella's heart was in her throat. With the certificate still in-hand, she raced toward the upstairs library, where Greta had always kept the family photo albums. Each of the children had their own, which charted the baby years, the toddler years, the scabbed knees, the gymnastics competitions, the piano recitals, the sleepovers, the baking parties, and so forth. Ella grabbed hers and whipped it open to the first page, where Greta held an infant Ella in her arms, all swaddled in blankets. Ella's face was impossibly small, and she had an adorable tuft of black hair.

Beside the photograph, Greta had written: *"Home for the first time."*

Ella's head spun with questions. The next photographs were of Bernard holding a baby Ella, followed by a teeny-tiny Julia trying her best to hold Ella, but with Greta's help. Next, a proud-looking Quentin held her while Alana stood off to the left, clearly performing for the camera.

It seemed that the Copperfields had been very present for Ella's first few days.

Was it possible that this birth certificate was a hoax? Some-one's idea of a joke? What?

Ella then grabbed Quentin's photo album and flipped to the first page. Here, Bernard had apparently done his best to record everything about Quentin's first few hours. There, an infant Quentin lay in a hospital crib. There, Greta lay in a hospital gown with Quentin across her chest. There, Bernard wore a hospital cap and held his first child for the first time.

They'd been at the hospital.

Ella flipped through Alana and Julia's photo albums after that and discovered that there, too, Bernard and Greta had recorded the very early moments of their children's lives at the hospital. Bernard, who'd always called himself a "photography buff," hadn't waited a single moment.

Why, then, had they waited till Ella had gotten home to start photographing?

Ella's knees clacked together. Slowly, she put each photo album back on the bookshelf, grabbed the copy of the birth certificate for Ella Blackwood from the library desk, and walked like a zombie to her mother's bedroom. This was the same bedroom she'd taken over after Bernard's sentencing, the same one Ella had entered and exited with dinners and breakfasts that Greta mostly refused to eat.

Here, Ella knocked on Greta's door.

Unlike all those years ago, Greta called, "Come in!"

Ella took a deep breath, telling herself that there had to be an explanation. Her world would go on spinning the way it always had been. She stepped through the door and found her mother at her own desk, a computer opened in front of her. She wore her cat-eyeglasses and seemed hard at work on something. An article? A manuscript? It warmed Ella's heart to know that her mother still had some creativity within her. Maybe their family coming together again had coaxed it back to life.

When Greta turned back to greet Ella, she caught sight of the copy of the birth certificate. "What's that?" She reached out and tugged it from Ella's hands, then stared at it for an impossible length of time. All the color drained from Greta's face. When she returned her gaze to Ella's, the sincere shock and fear that echoed back told Ella everything she needed to know.

Ella took a large step back. She was wordless.

"Ella, please. Let me explain."

Ella's heart exploded. She didn't want to hear any sort of explanation, not from a woman and a family that seemed entirely built on lies. She whirled around and rushed into the hallway, only grabbing her purse, keys, and guitar from her bedroom. As Greta called her name from the stairwell, she fled The Copperfield House, jumped into her station wagon, and started the engine.

Nothing would ever be all right again. That much was clear.

Chapter Fourteen

Ella parked her station wagon outside Nantucket High School. It was now two-twenty-five, which meant that high school wouldn't finish for the day for another thirty-five minutes. That wouldn't do. Feeling manic, Ella hopped out of the car and rushed into the front office, where the woman behind the desk said, "Good afternoon! How can I help you?"

Ella forced a smile. "Hi. My name is Ella Copperfield, and I need to take my son, Danny Ashton, out of school for the day. It's a private family matter."

The woman nodded, typed a message to herself on her computer, scribed a note on a little pad of paper, and then instructed Ella to sit and wait. "I'll go grab him from seventh period," she explained. "We won't be long."

Ella couldn't sit. She paced the office, blinking back tears. Childhood memories rushed through her mind. Bernard and Greta, who she'd once considered "the world's greatest parents," had seemingly adopted her. But why? And why hadn't they bothered to tell her? Ella began to connect other dotes, like Bernard's crimes. Liars were always liars, no matter what. Ella had learned that in the music industry; she'd also learned it within her "family."

"Hi, buddy!" Ella sounded insane as she greeted Danny, who looked petrified.

"Mom, is everything okay?" Danny placed his textbooks on the office desk and dropped down to hug his shorter mother.

Ella couldn't help it. She shook in her son's arms. *I gave birth to this baby. I remember the moment I first held him in my arms. That moment changed my life. Who, then, was Joni Blackwood? Did she still remember the first moment she held Ella?*

"I'll explain later," Ella said as she jumped out of Danny's embrace. "You have everything?"

Back in the station wagon, Ella donned her cat-eye sunglasses and thrust her foot on the gas pedal so hard that the tires squealed. Danny buckled himself in a split-second too late and said, "Mom? What's gotten into you?"

Ella's smile stretched from cheek to cheek. In a flash, they were at the Nantucket Harbor, where a ferry awaited to swallow up their car. This was perfect timing.

"Mom, I'm going to miss football practice," Danny pointed out.

"Jeremy said you could miss a day or two," Ella responded simply.

Danny seemed to know better than to bicker with his mother. As they inched up the ramp and into the belly of the ferry, Ella's phone began to buzz. As it was out between Danny and Ella, Danny was able to say, "You want me to get it? It's just Grandma."

"No. Don't." Ella swallowed the lump in her throat as Danny gave her a dangerous side-eyed glance. "I mean, there's nothing wrong," Ella tried to explain. "I'll call her back later. That's all."

Danny rolled his eyes slightly, clearly confused. Ella parked the car deep in the ferry, grabbed her phone, and then popped out into the dank air beneath the upper decks of the ship. Once there, her phone began to buzz again, this time with a call from Julia.

Ella's ears rang. Had they all been in on it? Had everyone known that she wasn't "one of the Copperfields"? Had this been why she'd always felt like such an outsider as a kid?

Oh, but how ironic that they'd all left her behind. The only non-Copperfield child, left back in the rotting Copperfield House to care for Greta alone. She should be angry! She should never speak to these people again!

Was she being rash? Her heart was shattered, and her brain seemed to latch onto an infinite number of possible, horrible realities. Just then, Alana began to call her, and Ella made a gut-wrenching decision to turn off her phone. She knew the drive back to the city like the back of her hand. It wouldn't be a problem.

Up on the top deck, Ella gripped the railing and stared back at the rock in the middle of the ocean, the one she'd planned to call "home" again. According to her birth certificate, she'd been born there, at Nantucket Cottage Hospital, just like her siblings. Why had Greta and Bernard brought her back to The Copperfield House?

Why couldn't Joni have taken her with her? Perhaps then, she would have avoided all that heartache. Then again, perhaps she never would have met Will, had her music career, or given birth to her own beautiful children. Gosh, her head and her heart couldn't make sense of anything. She pressed her palms against her eyes and willed herself not to scream.

Throughout this time, Danny had remained in the station wagon. When Ella returned to the driver's seat, he said, "I really don't mind missing practice. I just wish you'd tell me what's going on."

To this, Ella answered brightly, "We haven't seen your sister in ages. I thought we could surprise her."

Ella's only instinct was to draw her loved ones close and hold them until the pain went away. Surely, the pain would go away once she had Danny and Laura in her arms again. *Wouldn't it?*

"I hope you're ready to show me all your favorite new songs," Ella said to Danny as they raced back toward Manhattan, where Laura now lived in university housing.

Danny shrugged, clearly grateful to play DJ. He flipped through his Spotify until he came up with a post-punk band that Ella thought was vaguely cool and maybe something she would have liked back in the old days of her music career.

"Hey, bud?" Ella asked as they continued to race. "Would you mind Googling a name for me?"

"Sure. Is it a musician or something?"

"Yeah. I think so," Ella lied. "Joni Blackwood? Joni spelled like Joni Mitchell."

Ella held her breath as Danny typed the name into the search engine. "Huh. There are a lot of Joni Blackwoods. Any other information about her to narrow it down?"

"Nah. It's okay. I can look later."

Danny's eyes glittered with curiosity. "A really obscure musician, I guess?"

"You know me, bud," Ella tried to joke. "I only like bands that nobody has heard of."

"We know how pretentious you are," Danny quipped. "Laura calls you the first hipster."

"Does she?" Ella tried to laugh, but it sounded all wrong.

They reached Manhattan directly at rush hour. With enhanced concentration, Ella braked quickly, surged forward when she could, and finally discovered a near-perfect parking spot only three blocks from Columbia University's student housing. About an hour before, Danny had checked the class schedule that Laura had shared with both Danny and Ella, which showed that she would be leaving Havemeyer Hall at approximately seven-fifteen. Ella's stomach simmered with excitement. She was reminded of the days when she and Will had been on tour when they'd played a gig and immediately gotten into the van to take off for someplace else. Things had gotten rough in Nantucket— but they'd escaped. Maybe they wouldn't ever go back.

A stream of hundreds of students escaped Havemeyer Hall from seven to seven-fifteen. Ella and Danny waited expectantly off to the side, both feeling silly for separate reasons. Ella felt too old to be on a campus like this, surrounded by young people on the brink of the rest of their lives. Danny probably felt too young to be there, a foolish high school senior who couldn't measure up.

But then, like a ray of sunshine, Laura stepped out from Havemeyer Hall. Her hair whipped around in the September evening wind, and she was bundled up in a coat Ella had gotten on clearance and a scarf that Ella didn't recognize. She was in conversation with another young woman about her age, both with book bags across their shoulders. Danny lifted his arm and waved like an airplane operator, and suddenly, Laura's eyes widened with shock.

"What are you doing here?" she cried as she rushed toward them.

The view of her daughter running toward her was perfect. Ella's heart shattered with a mix of sorrow and joy as Laura wrapped her arms around her and held her close. She then hugged her brother with tears running down her cheeks.

"I'm sorry. I don't know why I'm crying," Laura rasped.

But Ella was crying too, of course. She hugged Laura another time, linked her arm with hers, and said, "We just couldn't wait to see you again."

"It's true," Danny chimed in, clearly pleased to be back in

the city and back with his sister. "I had no idea that life without you would be so boring."

"Ha. And that's coming from the football star of Nantucket High," Laura teased him.

"Your brother is something else on the field," Ella explained.

"I'll believe it when I see it," Laura said conspiratorially.

Laura had to drop off her backpack at her dorm. After that, the three of them would head out for a dinner that Ella probably couldn't totally afford. When night fell, she wasn't sure what she would say. Where would she and Danny sleep? Hotels in Manhattan were exorbitant. Airbnbs were probably out of the question.

For now, she decided to shove the question out of her mind. She wanted to enjoy the next several hours with her babies. She wanted to remember what it felt like to stand on solid ground.

"Oh, there's this insane new Vietnamese place we could check out," Laura explained as they stepped into the elevator of her university dorm. "Or a taco place that I really love. Their guacamole is to die for."

"It all sounds great." Ella's smile had begun to hurt her face.

"Nantucket has great restaurants, though," Danny began to say. "I was surprised."

"You're becoming an islander," Laura teased.

"I don't know about that," Danny returned.

The elevator door burst open to reveal the long hallway that led to Laura's dorm room. There, beside the very door that led into Laura's dorm room, stood a very familiar man. Ella's heart stopped beating. As her children tore down the hallway, calling out, "Dad! Oh my gosh. Dad!" Ella remained in the elevator. Everything about this day felt like a nightmare.

Will turned and smiled that ridiculously handsome smile at his children. He extended his arms out and hugged them with his eyes closed. Just as the elevator doors began to close, Ella forced herself to step into the hallway, where she walked toward her family with her arms crossed tightly over her chest.

"Mom, why didn't you tell us that Dad was coming?" Danny demanded. He looked just as happy as he had on his birthday as a child.

Ella lifted her left shoulder. "I wanted it to be a surprise."

"Oh. I can't even..." Laura blinked back tears as she removed her key from her pocket and let her family into her dorm room. "Just let me put my stuff away, and then we can head out to dinner."

Once inside the dorm room, Ella felt stifled by the smell of girls' cologne and girls' lotion and girls' semi-dirty clothing. Danny and Laura chatted amicably as Will and Ella remained near the door. Ella burned with desire to ask Will what the heck he was doing there. But when she turned to face him, the look in his eyes stopped her in her tracks.

There was something clearly wrong.

Finally, Will whispered, "It's nice to be all together again. Isn't it?"

"All right. Let's go!" Laura cried before Ella could answer, turning back from her desk.

"Whoop!" Danny's voice echoed down the hall.

Chapter Fifteen

Ella had never lived such a whirlwind of a day. Within the hour, she found herself seated at a four-top at a recent pop-up restaurant just east of Central Park. The restaurant, called "Cincos," had been decorated like the inside of a Mexican taqueria and sold traditional Mexican fare but still offered plenty of TexMex-style food to make Will happy, as he was often not as daring in the food department as the rest of his family.

Laura and Danny ordered water and cokes. When it came time for her turn, Ella basically yelped, "A margarita. Please." It sounded like her life depended on it. "Sorry," she added, trying to laugh. "I had a hard drive today."

"Driving makes me cranky, too," the waiter told her warmly before turning toward Will. "And you, sir? Something to drink?"

"I'll go with a margarita, too," Will said, offering Ella a smile. "Sounds tasty."

After they ordered enough quesadillas, tacos, chimichangas, and burritos to feed a small country, the waiter arrived with the margaritas and the cokes and left the family alone to talk amongst themselves. Ella was overwhelmed with all that she wanted to say and all she felt she couldn't say.

"Honey, you look fantastic!" Will said to Laura, squeezing her hand over the table. "How's your freshman year going?"

"Gosh, it's not easy." Laura's eyes were buggy. "We're only a few weeks in, and I already feel like my course load is insane. I did my first all-nighter the other night, and I'm still recovering."

"An all-nighter?" Ella asked.

Will intercepted this. "I think that's when college students stay up all night cramming for a test or writing a paper. Right?"

"That's it," Laura said with a smile.

"Wow." Ella and Will locked eyes for a moment, both probably thinking the same thing. The only "all-nighters" they'd known back then were the ones that involved all nights of playing music, listening to music, talking to other musicians, and drinking beer. Ella was proud of how different her children were than she and Will had been.

Laura continued to chat about her classes and the people she'd met. By the time the food arrived, Will had turned his attention to Danny, who described his time on the football team, his new friendship with his Grandpa Bernard, and the fact that "Nantucket really isn't that boring."

"I should say not," Will said with a laugh as he grabbed a chip from the bowl in the center. "Despite what some people say, New York City isn't the only place in the world. Nantucket has a pretty amazing history and is gorgeous to boot."

"Yeah, the history is insane. Mom's working on the Nantucket Jubilee, which celebrates two hundred years after... something happened." Danny pondered for a moment and crunched through a chip.

Will's beautiful eyes turned toward Ella for answers. "I take it you know what the Nantucket Jubilee celebrates?"

115

"Yes." Ella sipped her margarita, grateful to have that as an emotional crutch. "In the year 1820, a whaling ship called The Heart of Nantucket embarked on a whaling expedition but was soon said to be lost at sea. Families mourned the whalers they'd lost until two years later, in 1822, when The Heart of Nantucket returned."

"That's quite a story," Will said softly.

The waiter arrived with their plates of steaming, cheesy food. Ella dropped her gaze to the table and listened as her family chatted excitedly about their selections. This night felt just like hundreds of other nights across the span of her and Will's relationship and the building of their family. It was remarkable that it was so many months after she'd asked Will to leave.

After she'd scraped her plate clean, Laura recognized a friend in the corner. "She's in my History class," she explained, tugging Danny's elbow. "You should come to meet her."

"Why?" Danny asked.

Laura groaned. "You want me to say it? Okay, I'll say it. I miss you, and I do talk about you to my new friends. Okay? You happy? Now, let's go."

Laura and Danny laughed gently as they headed toward the corner to greet the young woman with the dreadlocks, who shook Danny's hand like a businesswoman. Now, Ella and Will sat alone at the table, at a loss for words and no longer able to lean on their children for guidance.

Finally, Ella dropped her fork against the side of her half-eaten meal and whispered, "All right. Tell me what's going on."

Will stiffened. Tenderly, he tapped a napkin over his lips and muttered, "I should say the same thing to you."

Ella's eyesight was blurry with tears. After a long pause, she stuttered, "You were just standing in Laura's dorm. Why?"

Will stuttered. "Your sisters wouldn't stop calling me!"

Ella's jaw dropped. "What did they say?"

"They said that something had gone wrong. That you'd gotten into a fight with your mother," Will explained.

"A fight? They called it a fight?" Ella bristled.

"They were really vague about everything," Will affirmed. "But they mentioned that you'd pulled Danny out of school early, and they had a hunch you were headed back home. To the city, that is."

Ella's cheeks burned. Without fully realizing what she wanted to say, she opened her lips and began to speak. "All I want in the world is to go back home to Brooklyn and crawl under the covers and cry and cry and cry."

Ella continued to stare at the table, terrified at her own words. But before she could start fully sobbing, Will's hand found hers on the table. His thumb traced the soft skin of her hand.

"I just never should have gone back there," Ella breathed. "I knew better than to trust those people."

"Your family?" Will sounded doubtful.

Ella's eyes flashed. "You know as well as I do what they've put me through the past twenty-five years." She swallowed the lump in her throat, then added, "And on top of it all, I just found out I'm not really one of them."

Will's face contorted. "What are you talking about?"

Ella bit her tongue and glanced toward her children, who remained in conversation with the young woman with dreadlocks. "Today, a mail courier came to The Copperfield House and delivered me a manila envelope. Inside, I found a copy of a birth certificate for someone named Ella Blackwood, born June 12, 1980."

Will's jaw dropped. Under his breath, he whispered, "Did it seem legitimate?"

Ella continued to speak quickly, wanting to get it all out before her children returned. "At first, I was wary. But then, I checked out my siblings' photo albums, which all included photos right after delivery in the hospital. Mine doesn't have any. I became suspicious, so I knocked on Greta's door. The look on Greta's face told me everything I needed to know. So, I ran out of the house, picked up Danny, and now, I'm here."

"At Cincos," Will finished.

"At Cincos."

Will looked flabbergasted. He rubbed his hands over his beard and repeated, "Oh my gosh," a few times, as though that meant anything. He then said, "I guess I would have done the same thing as you. I would have wanted Danny and Laura close."

"And here we are together," Ella whispered, her voice breaking.

* * *

Later that evening, Will, Ella, and Danny dropped Laura back off at her dorm and then jumped in Ella's station wagon to head to the apartment that Will now subleased from a friend. Ella had only ever been there back in the old days, when she and Will had been together, and the place had just been "a friend's place." Now, it seemed to symbolize so much pain.

The apartment was small, with a bedroom, a small office with a twin-sized bed, and a living room with a television and a couch. As they entered, Will placed his keys on the kitchen counter like he owned the place and said, "Tonight, I'll be sleeping on the couch."

"Oh, you don't have to do that," Ella said.

Will's expression meant business. "That's the way we're going to do it. No arguments."

Danny was only moderately impressed with the apartment, as it didn't have the same memories as their old place and barely had a view of the street below. Of course, he soon discovered Will's friend's record collection and dove through memory lane, blaring Sonic Youth and My Blood Valentine albums like there was no tomorrow. Will and Ella sat in the kitchen with glasses of wine and listened as the songs roared in from the living room.

"I'm so angry for you," Will said suddenly, surprising Ella.

"What do you mean?"

Will shook his head. "You discovered this enormous family secret so late in life. How do you even begin to grapple with that? How do you begin to move ahead when you now have so many questions?"

Ella was speechless. These were all questions that had hummed through her head all day.

"I want to go back to Nantucket with you," Will said firmly. "I want to help you through this."

Ella locked eyes with him, willing herself to say no. Things were over between Ella and Will; she'd known that for months.

"What about the tour?" Ella asked.

Will spread his fingers out across the table. "We're on a break right now, with two months of downtime. I'm getting bored hanging around New York City by myself."

Ella wanted to point out that already, he'd suggested that they should date other people. She held it back, pleased he'd been bored without her.

"Besides, this is bigger than the tour," Will continued. "Like it or not, you've been my ride-or-die since I was nineteen years old. No matter what stage our relationship is at, I'd still like to think we can be there for each other. I'd still like to think that you're my best friend in the world."

Ella closed her eyes against his intensity, overwhelmed. He was so clearly the man she'd met at eighteen, the one she'd felt comfortable enough with to talk to all night and into the next morning. He'd been the first person who'd ever really listened to her.

She'd been silent too long. Will had grown jittery. As Ella

pulled open her eyes to speak, Will sputtered, "And I'm sorry I got a drink with that Marcia Conrad lady."

Somehow, Ella had almost forgotten about that. "Oh..."

"It's just that I was lonely, she really wanted to go out, and I was so tired of sitting in my hotel room by myself after gigs," Will continued. "The entire time I was there, I wanted to be with you. It felt insane that I wasn't with you."

Will staggered to a halt, perhaps realizing that he'd gone too far. *Had both of them gone too far at this point?* It had been such an emotional day.

"It's okay." Ella swallowed the lump in her throat. "Marcia Conrad is a complicated person in my family's life. But that's a story for another time." At this point, Ella wasn't even sure she cared about Marcia Conrad. Her world had been turned on its head.

After another dramatic pause, Will spoke.

"Your family owes you an explanation. And I'd like to help you through it. If you'd let me."

In the next room, "London Calling" from The Clash roared from the speakers. Both Ella and Will could feel Danny's ecstasy about the music.

"He plays football now. I can't believe it," Ella said instead of answering Will.

Will laughed, his face opening up joyfully. "Our kids are many things," he said finally. "They have so much of us in them, but they are also uniquely themselves. Isn't that the greatest gift of all?"

Ella's eyes filled with tears. She knew he was right.

"I would love you to come with me," Ella breathed. "On Nantucket, I was learning to find ways to ask for help. And now, here I am, telling you that I don't think I can do any of this alone."

Chapter Sixteen

F riday morning, Ella awoke in Will's friend's bed as the gray light of the last day of September shimmered through the blinds. In the next rooms, Will and Danny slept on, their snores rising and falling like the tides.

It was seven, which meant that Danny was meant to be in school within the hour. As they were several hours away, that wasn't going to happen. Ella grabbed her phone and turned it back on, trying to ignore each message and missed call from her sisters and mother.

ALANA: I don't know what's going on, but Mom won't stop crying.

JULIA: Will you please call us back?

Ella spoke with the front desk secretary at the high school to explain that Danny had to miss school due to a "private family matter" but would be in attendance the following evening for the Nantucket High School versus Falmouth High School football game. Ella knew that Danny counted on being there. Despite her anxiety about returning to the island, she wanted to get back there for him.

Ella walked into the kitchen and began to brew a pot of coffee. Outside, a blissful New York City autumn day crept open, with beautiful coffeeshops opening out across the sidewalks, trendy-looking hipsters walking past in autumnal hats, and several musician-types carrying guitars and other instruments over their shoulders. This was the life Ella had once known. Now, she felt caught between worlds.

By the time Will and Danny got up, Ella had a full breakfast spread of bagels and different types of cream cheeses set up across the kitchen table.

"That is one thing about Nantucket," Danny said sleepily as he selected an Everything Bagel. "The bagels just don't compare to the cities."

"You got that right," Will said as he scratched his head adorably. "That's one of the hardest things about the tour. In fact, your mom and I used to make that our first stop when we got back to the city."

"Bagels?" Danny asked with a mischievous grin.

"You bet your bottom dollar," Will said.

Together, the three of them sat with their bagels and contemplated what to do next. Ella suggested that they hit up the Metropolitan Museum of Art, as she hadn't been there in years, and both guys agreed whole-heartedly.

"Now that I'm an All-American jock, I need a bit of artistic input every now and then," Danny joked.

Ella and Will exchanged glances and burst into laughter. After a moment, Will added, "I hope you don't mind that I'll be at your game tomorrow night."

Danny's face glowed with surprise. After a moment, he forced his lips closed and said, "Oh, cool," like he didn't care at all. Both Will and Ella knew just how much it meant to him, though.

* * *

By the time the three of them boarded Ella's station wagon the following late morning, they'd fallen even more in-sync with one another. They cracked family jokes that they hadn't heard in years and ate snacks they'd always loved— Nutter Butter Peanut Butter Cookies, Pizza-Flavored Combos, and Will and Danny's favorite, Pork Rinds.

"Any other family would think we're disgusting," Danny pointed out from the back seat, clearly pleased that he had his parents to himself.

"We'd better brush our teeth before we see anyone else in public," Ella pointed out, where she sat in the passenger seat, allowing Will to drive. It felt so wonderful to have him there, picking up the slack like this. They'd hardly had any physical contact at all, but just the sound of his voice and the sturdiness of his hands across the wheel felt like enough just then.

The station wagon wheeled off the ferry and onto Nantucket at four-forty-five that afternoon. Ella's stomach curdled with panic as she had no idea where she wanted to stay that night. She didn't feel up to explaining the situation to Danny, at least not yet. But that meant she and Will had to pretend that everything was mostly okay, both between them and between Ella and the rest of the family.

When they reached The Copperfield House, Danny popped out, grabbed his textbooks, and headed inside.

"Hey, honey?" Ella called from the passenger window as Danny tried to disappear into the massive Victorian house. "We're going to run some errands, okay? We'll see you up at the football field."

"Cool," Danny said easily. "See ya."

With Danny inside, Will shook his head playfully and said, "The kid is cooler than I ever was. That's for sure." After a pause, he added, "And he hasn't had any trouble with, you know..."

Ella knew that Will meant "drinking." She shook her head and eyed her knees.

"Taking him away from all that was the right thing," Will said softly. "Thank you for doing that." After another pause, he added, "You're such a wonderful mother. I hope you know that."

Ella blinked back tears, willing herself to pull herself together. She then instructed Will to head to the Nantucket Inn, where she'd booked them one room with two twin beds. There, they could consider what to do next. There, she could pull herself together, even as she acknowledged the weight of what she'd just learned.

Once inside the hotel room, Ella sat at the edge of one of the twin beds and began to strum the guitar that she'd grabbed before she'd fled The Copperfield House. Will leaned against the wall, watching the autumn leaves whip around in the breeze outside the window. Ella strummed the guitar thoughtfully. How many times had she and Will played music together? *How many times had they messed around on guitars together before ultimately discovering their "brand-new song"?*

"I'm going to take a shower," Will said, scrubbing his hand through his dark hair.

"Okay." Ella sensed that he felt the emotion of the music just as much as she did. Maybe he missed playing music with her just as much as she did, too.

The Nantucket football game was set for seven that evening. Bundled up in autumn jackets and scarves, Ella and Will walked a full foot apart, entering the throng of football fans, parents, and bright-faced high schoolers. It was hard to believe that Will and Ella had been that young when they'd met. Ella thought about talking about the fact that she, Stephanie, and Brenda had snuck off the island for one wild night in Greenwich Village, the night that had changed her life forever, but she soon thought better of it. Will asked if she wanted to share a bucket of popcorn, and she agreed.

Once in the stands, Will sat pin-straight and gazed out across the field at his son, who was all dressed up in his football jersey, pads, and a helmet. "It's wild to see him like that," Will muttered, digging into the bucket of popcorn and chewing slowly.

"It freaked me out the first time," Ella admitted.

Will turned and shared a secret smile. "It's like we're small-town parents."

"I sort-of am, now," Ella countered. "I went to a PTA meeting the other day at Danny's school."

"You're kidding."

Ella shook her head, sharing in Will's laughter. "Bye, bye, rock star days," she joked.

Will's face darkened earnestly. "Don't say that."

Ella shrugged. "It's true."

"No." Will shook his head, his smile falling. "You're a world-class musician. Just because you've taken time off to care for our children doesn't mean that your rock star days are through."

"Will, come on. I'm forty-two years old. A woman's shelf-life in the music world is much shorter than a man's," Ella said simply.

Will continued to shake his head, clearly wanting to argue. But before he could, the man behind the microphone announced that the game was about to begin. Ella told Will to "pay attention." As she turned her head to watch the opening play, she spotted Alana, Julia, and Greta down on the second row of the stands, all bundled up in a blanket.

The Copperfield Women.

Ella's heart shattered at the realization that she was no longer, nor had never really been, one of them. Had they seen her? They knew she was back, surely, since Danny was out on the field. Ella blinked back the tears and listened as, beside her, Will howled, "Let's go, Danny!"

Although Ella wasn't exactly a sports fanatic, the game was spectacular. Falmouth and Nantucket played neck-in-neck throughout the first three quarters until Nantucket managed to edge Falmouth out with a final score of 27-24. Both Ella and Will leaped to their feet, yelling along with the rest of the Nantucketers. Will's face exuded joy.

By the time Ella and Will reached the field to congratulate Danny, Danny was already surrounded by Greta, Alana, and Julia. Jeremy clapped Danny on the back and loudly said, "I swear, if you hadn't moved to Nantucket this autumn, we wouldn't have had a chance." Both Alana and Julia beamed as Greta stepped forward and tried to wrap her thin arms around the bulky pads of Danny's uniform.

Ella and Will stood several feet away, unsure of where to go or what to do. Midway through his hug with Greta, Danny spotted them and waved them over, oblivious. Will forced himself forward and hugged Danny excitedly, saying, "You killed it out there, man." Ella limped up behind him and waited for her turn to hug Danny, avoiding her sisters' and mother's gazes. The intensity was too great.

"Why don't we all go home?" Greta announced. "I have a bunch of party foods all prepped. Danny, maybe you would like to invite a few of your teammates?"

Danny flashed Greta an All-American smile. "Sure. We can come for a while. After that, I promised my new buddy, Kyle, that I'd come over for a little get-together." He then met Ella's gaze to add a serious, "It's not a party. I promise."

"Fantastic!" Greta said, clasping her hands together. She then turned to speak to both Will and Ella. "I expect both of you back at the house, as well." Her words were scary and final. There was no getting out of it.

Back in Ella's station wagon, Ella groaned. "I guess tonight is as good a time as any to get to the bottom of this."

"Let's just celebrate Danny's win, meet his new friends, and then see how we feel," Will said coaxingly. "Nobody's going to force you to have that conversation today. I understand how insane it must feel to go back."

Ella blinked back tears, overwhelmed with how good Will was at handling her moods and her feelings. For the first time in many years, a thought sprung up in the back of her mind. *I don't deserve him.*

Back at The Copperfield House, Greta had already lined nachos, quesadillas, chicken wings, spinach and artichoke dip, and a big vat of clam chowder across the back porch table. It was October, and a pregnant moon hung low in the night sky. Out on the closed porch, Greta, Alana, Julia, Ella, Will, Danny, and two of Danny's friends from the football team remained warm, even as a Nantucket wind blasted against the glass. For the better part of the next two hours, Danny and his friends talked about the ins-and-outs of the game, how they'd managed to score the last few goals, approaching sectionals, followed by regionals, and their hope for state finals.

Throughout, a terrible tension existed between Ella and Greta. Ella could hardly look at her. She nibbled at the edge of a chicken wing and grew frightened at how angry she really felt. What could she do with that anger? It wasn't useful. It just ate her up inside.

Danny and his friends left around eleven-thirty. Alana admitted to having a late-night date with Jeremy at his place, while Julia said she had to get some shut-eye if she wanted to do any editing the next day. After everyone said "goodnight" and "goodbye," only Greta, Will, and Ella remained on the back porch, separated by mounds of leftover food.

"I'll clean up," Ella said suddenly, reaching for the big tray of nachos and heading inside. The tension made the air impossible to breathe.

"Ella, wait." Greta grabbed the vat of clam chowder and headed in after her.

Ella reached the kitchen with both Greta and Will hot on her heels. Ella placed the nachos on the counter, crossed her arms, and began to head back toward the porch to continue to clean. But before she could, Greta screeched, "Won't you please let me explain myself?"

Ella spun on her heel and gaped at the woman she'd always thought to be her mother— the woman she'd had to fight to keep alive back in her teenage years. "I don't know if I have time for that," Ella returned. "This family has been nothing but heartache for me for twenty-five years. And now, it turns out that you're not my family at all? That my life has been a lie?"

Greta's eyes glittered with sorrow. Slowly, she backed up to the kitchen table, where she grabbed a regular envelope that was yellowed with time. She then pointed toward the kitchen chairs and said, "Give me five minutes. Please."

Ella lifted her eyes toward Will's, terrified. She never should have come back here. Will placed a hand on her shoulder and gave her the same look he'd given her thousands of times before a concert. The look had always told her: *It's going to be okay. We're going to get through this.*

Ella and Will sat across from Greta, who fumbled with the unsealed top of the envelop and eventually removed a stack of old photographs. On the back, Greta's beautiful calligraphy had scribed words that looked like: **JONI B 1980**. A cold shiver ran up and down Ella's spine.

Greta passed the stack over to Ella. Quietly, Greta watched as Ella flipped through the photographs. Each featured a very young and very pregnant young woman with dark hair and clever eyes. In multiple photographs, Joni Blackwood strummed a guitar and sang with whoever sat around her, attractive men and women wearing seventies- and eighties-style clothing. In some, she was alone, often on the beach with her hand across her pregnant stomach.

The photographs were heartbreaking. They told a story of a woman who'd loved music with all her heart and mind, just as Ella always had. Ella found herself carving out a space in her heart for Joni Blackwood, even though she knew little more about her than these photographs.

"She came to The Copperfield House's residency program when she was six months pregnant," Greta began softly. "In her application, she hadn't mentioned the pregnancy, so that was a bit of a surprise for your father and I when she arrived. She'd said that she was working on a folk album and wanted the space and time to do that somewhere. She'd also sent along a recording of her work, which your father and I loved. Gosh, she was talented. Her voice was raspy and soulful, and her guitar playing rivaled Jimi Hendrix's, I swear."

Ella and Will exchanged glances. The "past tense" in Greta's words terrified Ella.

"I had three little kids at the time," Greta continued. "Julia was almost one, and Alana and Quentin weren't too much older than that. Because Joni was such a sweet soul, she often helped me around the house with the children. Through that, we became friends. When that friendship grew deeper, she broke down to tell me that she didn't have enough money to care for her baby, that she still wanted to go after her music dreams, and that she hated that her baby didn't have a father."

Ella's mouth was terribly dry. Will rubbed her lower back knowingly, trying to tell her that he was still there, supporting her.

"Eventually, Bernard and I talked over Joni's situation," Greta said. "We didn't feel right about knowingly putting Joni out on the streets when she was so pregnant. We decided that she would have the baby on Nantucket, where we could help her get a job, help out with childcare, and eventually send her back into the world with more money, more experience, and a better grip on her music career."

Greta's voice cracked as she continued. "You were born on July 12th, 1980. I was there at the hospital, helping Joni through. It was a difficult labor. She was terribly exhausted afterward and slept for the better part of three or four days. Things were different back then; they didn't diagnose things like Postpartum Depression. When she looked at you..."

Ella closed her eyes, unsure if she wanted to hear just how much her real mother hadn't loved her.

"She looked at you with all the love in the world," Greta finished. "But she admitted to me that she just couldn't do it. Not then." Greta swiped her hand across her cheek to mop up the tears. "After she left, she wrote letters for a little while. I managed to send her multiple photographs of you until her letters dried up, and I lost track of exactly where she was. I hoped she was still out there, making music. But I never heard about her or from her ever again."

Outside, an angry Nantucket wind barrelled against the side of The Copperfield House. Exhausted like a small child, Ella leaned her head on Will's shoulder and exhaled all the air from her lungs.

"I'm so sorry, honey," Greta continued. "Your father and I always meant to tell you. But suddenly, we got so wrapped up in our four children, our artist residency family, our friends, and our status in the community. It no longer seemed impor-tant that you weren't actually a 'Copperfield.' You even looked like Alana and Julia, to us, at least." Greta sniffed. "It felt like one of those lies you tell yourself until you believe it. And Ella..." Greta now looked stricken. "You were the only one of my babies who came back sometimes over the years. Even as Julia and Quentin stayed away with their families, I was allowed to know Laura and Danny. That was the most remark-able gift in the world! I can't begin to thank you."

Ella's chin quivered with sorrow. Greta's story was a tragic one. It seemed almost unreal.

"Nothing could ever bring me to stop loving you," Greta blared then, finding more strength in her voice. "I hope you'll find a way to forgive all these stupid lies. It's like I keep telling your sisters. We have to find a way forward, with empathy and love."

Chapter Seventeen

Sleep was the furthest thing from Ella's mind. Back at the Nantucket Inn, she paced the little space between her and Will's twin beds with her hands latched behind her back. In the bathroom, Will brushed his teeth, and the sound was reassuring— a sound Ella had heard countless nights. Will was fastidious about his teeth, which wasn't exactly rock star behavior. It was, however, "father" behavior. Since becoming one, Will had become very much in tune with his body, saying, "I want to live as long as I can so that I can see my children and grandchildren grow up."

When Will emerged from the bathroom, he rubbed his hands through his lush hair and said, "There's no way you can sleep, right?"

Ella shook her head. "I don't think I'm going to try."

Will nodded contemplatively and dropped down to assess the mini bar. "Shouldn't have brushed my teeth," he muttered as he removed a bottle of red wine. With a swivel of the bottle opener, he yanked the cork out and poured them two cups in the plastic ones provided by the hotel. They then clinked their glasses together, nodded, and drank. Ella fell back on the edge of her bed, her head throbbing. The wine seemed necessary; maybe she would find a way to sleep.

After a long pause, Will spoke. "You remember that first night we met?"

Ella nodded, surprised.

"You told me so much about your family that night," Will said. "I remember listening to you talk about everything that had happened and thinking, 'Wow. This girl is one of the loneliest girls I've ever met.' I didn't feel sorry for you, of course. Instead, I just recognized that you knew how to use that pain and sorrow to make damn good music.

"Anyway. It's wild, remembering that story now, and realizing that it's just the tip of the iceberg," Will continued. "I can't imagine what you're feeling right now. I just want you to know that all of your feelings about it are valid. And I'm here, you know? I'm here for as long as you need me to be."

Ella's eyes filled with tears. Along the bedside table, she'd arranged the photographs of a pregnant Joni Blackwood, who peered out at the modern world with a sense of optimism.

"You were always my family, anyway, Will," Ella murmured, her words hardly audible even for herself.

Will held the silence for a long time before he managed to say, "It was just us against the world. Then, it was us, Laura, and Danny against the world."

"Things got a bit more complicated when the record company got so involved," Ella admitted, remembering the early fights about recording contracts and how often they could go on tour, given the fact that they had children.

"We really threw a wrench in their plan when we got pregnant," Will said mischievously.

"Gosh, can you imagine our lives without them?" Ella asked, suddenly aghast. "I remember once that seedy guy Greg who worked at the recording company asked if I would consider giving our baby up for adoption or pushing her off on a friend. He made it seem like it was impossible to make it in the music industry with a baby."

"You were so angry at him," Will breathed. "You refused to ever work with Greg again. At the time, that was all right. Our album sales were good enough that we could make up our own rules."

"It's wild that we ever lived that life," Ella whispered. "Although I guess, in some ways, you're still living that life. You're out on tour, playing to hundreds if not thousands of people. Gosh, I hate to say that I'm jealous." She dropped her gaze to the ground.

"I've told you before. It's not the same without you," Will said.

Ella wasn't sure how to respond, so for a stretch of minutes, no words were said.

"What do you think you'll do now?" Will asked.

"Gosh, I don't know." Ella hung her head. "I feel so displaced. The band broke up. We broke up. Laura's off to college. Danny's a football jock at Nantucket High. And I'm— the daughter of a folk musician who didn't want me?"

Will sipped his wine. "Have you looked her up?"

"Yeah. Several times. I searched 'Joni Blackwood - Musician' even before Greta told us that story because it just made sense that I had some kind of musician mother."

"Nothing came up?" Will asked.

"Nope. She's a mystery," Ella said. "I don't know what to make of that, either."

In the silence that followed, Will stepped through the space between their beds, sat a full foot away from her, and placed a gentle hand on her hand. Ella felt herself fold against him so that her head shivered with the thudding of his heart. This man was her man. This was her Will.

"I'm not going to take Danny out of school," Ella whispered. "He's already doing too well here."

Will nodded. "That's very kind of you."

"It's not even about kindness right now," Ella offered. "It's more about clinging to solid ground."

Will's voice cracked. "I can stay on the island till the end of the break in my tour."

Ella sniffed. "Thank you, Will. I don't think I can thank you enough." After another pause, she added, "But we have to stay at The Copperfield House. Danny will want us both there."

"Are you sure?" Will asked.

Ella nodded. "If you're there with me, I know I can make it through. Besides, I'm tired of running away from my problems. Maybe Greta is right. Maybe we can find a way forward, with empathy and love, no matter what."

Doubt edged Ella's voice and heart. Now that she'd lost everything, there wasn't anything else to lose.

Chapter Eighteen

T hat Monday morning, Stephanie was bug-eyed with
adrenaline and panic. "Oh my gosh. I'm so glad
you're here!" She raced up to Ella at the Nantucket
Community Music Center, grabbed her wrists, and said,
"Somebody said that you'd moved back to New York City, and
I almost had a heart attack. I thought, 'Right before the
Nantucket Jubilee? Is she insane?'"

Ella's nose twitched with annoyance. Nantucket Island was
a remarkable place with gorgeous coastlines, a marvelous
history, and a real obsession with gossip. Probably, somebody
had spotted her driving her station wagon onto the ferry and
sent a lie across the island like wildfire.

"No way, Steph. I wouldn't leave you high and dry like
that," Ella said.

"I should have known." Stephanie's laughter made her
sound like she was insane. "Are you ready to get started? I have
about forty-seven billion projects to complete before Friday."

Ella threw herself into the last week of Nantucket Jubilee

preparations with fanatical zeal, grateful to have something to take her mind off the panic of learning her real identity. Monday, Tuesday, and Wednesday nights that week, she returned to a mostly-dark Copperfield House and normally discovered Danny and Will in the upstairs living room, chilling in front of Will's computer and chatting about music. Those nights, she heated herself up some soup and sat with them, calmed by the rhythm of their voices.

On Wednesday evening, as Ella prepared for bed, Julia and Alana appeared at her bedroom door. Both had damaged eyes. Ella hadn't spoken to either of them much at all since the week before when she'd run out on their barbecue and fled the island.

"Can we talk?" Alana whispered.

Ella beckoned for them to enter her childhood bedroom. Together, the three of them sat cross-legged on the bed, waiting for the first to speak. Finally, Julia blurted out, "What's going on, Ella?"

Ella's thoughts staggered to a halt. She now recognized that both Alana and Ella's faces were marred with confusion and sorrow.

"You don't know?" Ella asked.

Both Alana and Julia shook their heads violently.

"Know what?" Alana demanded.

Ella heaved a sigh and hunted through her purse to discover the envelope filled with photographs of Joni. She then passed the envelope over and watched as her sisters' faces contorted with even more confusion.

"Who is this?" Julia demanded.

"She's my real mother," Ella recited, terrified at how easy it now was to say.

Julia and Alana's jaws dropped open.

"What are you talking about?" Julia shrieked.

"Shh." Ella took the photos back and glanced toward the

bedroom door. "I don't want to talk to Mom about this anymore. It was hell."

Alana and Julia ordered Ella to explain everything she now knew. Ella covered it as best as she could and then explained that the birth certificate had come in a manila envelope addressed to Ella at The Copperfield House the previous week. At this, Julia nearly flew off the handle.

"Who on earth knew about this?" she demanded.

Incredibly, this was the first time that Ella had considered this. *Who had sent the envelope? And why hadn't it had a return address?*

"Other people on the island obviously knew about it," Ella said finally. "Mom wasn't pregnant in 1980, and then suddenly, she had a brand-new baby."

"But Ella, even if they told everyone that they adopted you, who would go out of their way to send you that birth certificate?" Alana demanded.

Ella shrugged. "The Copperfields have enemies on this island. Maybe one of Dad's ex-friends wants to get his own revenge."

"Through you? That's messed up," Julia pointed out.

After another half-hour of whispered questions and shrugs of disbelief, Alana and Julia hugged Ella as hard as they could.

"I wish you would have told us what was going on," Alana said pointedly as she stood up from the bed, wincing after so long sitting cross-legged.

"Seriously, Sis," Julia said. "You didn't have to run off to New York City and leave us scratching our heads."

Before Ella could protest, Alana stammered, "And don't think for a second that this stupid piece of paper proves that you're not actually our sister."

Julia's nostrils flared angrily. Before Ella could protest again, Julia then whispered, with a sudden smile, "But Will's still here?"

Ella's cheeks grew warm with girlish embarrassment. It was as though they were teenagers all over again. "I mean, he just wants to hang out with Danny," she lied.

"The way he looks at you. That man doesn't want to go anywhere you're not going," Alana insisted.

"Our relationship is difficult to explain." Ella sounded timid. "Besides, when he heard about Joni Blackwood and all this drama, he knew I needed him. But he knows that I don't need him forever."

This was one of the biggest lies Ella had ever said aloud.

* * *

The following night, Ella returned to a dark Copperfield House at eight-thirty. It had been a terrifically difficult day in the world of the Nantucket Jubilee. The festival was set to begin the following afternoon, with an initial re-enactment of the arrival of The Heart of Nantucket, complete with appropriate costumes and a band that played the "top hits" of 1822. So far, multiple actors, writers, and musicians had arrived from across the United States and beyond, bringing with them multiple demands and multiple problems. Still, Stephanie assured Ella and the rest of the Nantucket Jubilee team that everything was off to a "great start."

Ella stood in the kitchen at the stovetop and flipped a grilled cheese. As her thoughts slowed and her anxiety lessened, she realized that there were voices coming from the back porch. Very soon, she realized that the voices were all male: Danny's, Will's, and, remarkably, Bernard's.

Ella stood in the shadows of the hallway with her grilled cheese sandwich lifted. Like a silly high schooler, she began to eavesdrop.

"Yeah, that last week, we were out in Seattle, Portland, San Francisco, and Los Angeles," Will explained his latest tour.

"San Francisco used to be such a great town," Bernard said, his words heavy with nostalgia. "That's on my list of places I'd like to visit now that I'm out."

"It's definitely changed over the years," Will countered. "Even back when Ella and I used to tour there in the 2000s, the crowd was different than it is today. The tech boom did a number on the city's culture."

"The tech boom!" Bernard chuckled to himself. "While I was away, I tried very hard to imagine how life would be once I got out. I have to admit that I was very wrong. I never could have imagined this 'tech boom.' I never could have imagined looking up anything you need to know at the drop of a hat. What was that website you showed me the other day, Danny?"

"Wikipedia," Danny chimed in. "It has everything."

Ella continued to listen, her grilled cheese untouched on her plate. Soon after, they reached the topic of what Bernard planned to do now that he was "free."

"I don't know how to feel about that word," Bernard said philosophically. "I don't believe that any of us are technically free, as we are parts of systems that are beyond our control. That said, I do have a life to live. A life that I will now think of as 'after prison.' And with that life, I haven't a clue what to do."

"I can imagine," Will said softly. "It must be a very difficult thing to think about, especially after you lost so much time."

"The artist residency sounded so cool," Danny offered. "You should open it back up again!"

"Ella always spoke highly of the artist residency," Will said. "She said you had a real talent for honing other people's talents."

Bernard barked with laughter. "I don't know about that. Maybe it was all in my head. Besides, if we reopened The Copperfield House Artist Residency, who would come? I'm infamous across the country. On top of it all, I'm pretty old and out of practice these days."

"Grandpa, you just wrote one of the top-selling books of the summer," Danny interjected.

"I wrote that over the span of a decade," Bernard insisted. After another pause, he added, "In any case, if we reopened the artist residency, I would need a great deal of help."

"Your daughters are all incredibly artistic," Will chimed in.

"True." Bernard sounded contemplative. "It would be good to have another musician, Will. If you get what I'm hinting at."

"Dad! You should totally work at the artist residency," Danny cried.

"I don't know." Will sounded both intrigued and frightened at the prospect.

"You wouldn't have to work all those bad jobs back in the city," Danny continued.

"I'll consider it if you consider it, Will." Bernard spoke of this as though it was a pipe dream. "But I know that your heart lies in touring, and we won't have you here at The Copperfield House for long, no matter how much Danny and I hope that you stay."

Ella's eyes filled with tears. Quickly, she rushed back toward the circular staircase and took the steps two at a time until she collapsed in her childhood bedroom. There, she pressed her face in her pillow and tried to imagine a beautiful future where she and Will kicked off the bad memories and started anew. Her imagination came up blank.

Chapter Nineteen

T hat night around ten-fifteen, there was a knock at Ella's bedroom door. Expecting no one but one of her sisters, she called out, "Come in," and continued to stand in only a tank top and shorts, her back to the door.

"Ella?" Will's voice was raspy and tentative.

Ella whipped around, flipping her dark hair along with her. She said a small prayer of thanks that she hadn't washed off her makeup yet. "Hi, Will." She swallowed the lump in her throat, then asked, "Are you okay? Do you need anything?"

Will lifted his shoulder and stepped into her bedroom. As he leaned against the wall, he said that he, Danny, and Bernard had spent the evening talking about life, love, philosophy, and some of the thoughts that Bernard had had while he'd been away. "It was heavy, to say the least," Will finished.

"It sounds like it," Ella said. On instinct, she stepped toward Will and placed a hand on his upper back. *When was the last time they'd kissed one another? Had they kissed the day he'd left the apartment the last time? Or had their final kiss been*

*random and instinctual, a goodnight kiss or a quick "see you
later" kiss?*

Ella's guitar lay across the bed. Since she'd retreated from
spying on the guys, all Ella had done was strum it, looking for a
sound she couldn't find. Ella watched Will as he stepped
forward, his arms drooping along his sides. Back in the old days,
when they'd had a problem that they couldn't work through,
they'd always taken that problem to their music. They'd written
some of their best albums that way.

"Come on," Ella breathed, grabbing the guitar from the
bed.

Will followed her wordlessly down the circular staircase
and then through the hallway that separated the artist residency from the family house. Ella knew the route to the music
practice room like the back of her hand. The room had been
her refuge back in her teenage years, as it was padded, and she
could play as long and as loudly as she'd wanted to. Often, she'd
been mistaken for a member of the artist residency by sound
alone until she'd stepped out and revealed herself to be a pre-
teenaged girl.

Ella opened the door of the practice room to discover that,
miraculously, a drum set remained, along with a collection of
drumsticks. Recently, the room had been cleaned, probably by
either Julia or a cleaning team she'd hired during her revamp of
The Copperfield House. There in the practice room, Ella felt
as though she'd stepped back in time.

Above the padding of the wall, Bernard had hung shelves
that now carried a number of trophies and photographs from
previous attendees of The Copperfield House Residency. One
of the photographs also featured Ella, seated on a table in the
garage with a guitar across her lap. Ella hadn't seen that photograph in years.

"Not a bad set," Will said as he sat and adjusted the drum
seat beneath him.

Ella swung the strap of her guitar over her shoulder. They shared a timid smile just as Ella's anxiety grew. Will and Ella had played thousands of hours of music together. But what would they play next? Perhaps they'd lost their "magic"?

"Let's play one of the old ones," Will said suddenly. "I feel nostalgic."

They agreed to play "New In Town," a song they'd written during the summer of 2002 when Brooklyn had felt especially stifling with humidity. Ella half-remembered figuring out the chords and the lyrics of the song in a single afternoon. After that, she and Will had played it at nearly every concert, as it had been a fan favorite.

Ella and Will could have played that song in their sleep. As they breezed through it, singing harmonies, Ella's heart lifted with happiness. This was it; this was the version of them that she'd missed so much.

After "New In Town," they continued to play the hits from the old days, including some of the songs they'd written in honor of their children's births: "Laura, Open Your Eyes," and "Danny In The Morning," both of which had been adored by fans. Will and Ella had always been very private about their family life, yet their love for their children had always bled through their music.

Forty-five minutes in, Will asked Ella if she wanted to start improvising and "work on new stuff." Ella, caught up in the moment, agreed and began to fiddle around with new chords and new scales. Will followed along easily. It was like they played as one.

Soon, their music became louder and more frantic. It was as though all the chaos of the past year of fighting came through in their music. Will banged the drums as loud as he could. His eyes were manic. Ella's fingers made the guitar shriek. It was more intense than any live performance they'd ever played—and it was only meant for them.

It was as though they were finally able to say all the things they'd wanted to say.

But suddenly, one side of a shelf burst off from the wall and swung down against the wall padding. The movement of the solid piece of wood falling made Ella whip around and gape. Will stopped playing, and for a little while, their ears rang and rang.

"Did we just break that shelf by playing too loudly?" Will asked, his eyes twinkling.

Ella laughed and laughed. She felt like a teenager again, overwhelmed with the power of music. She then swung the guitar from her shoulders, locked eyes with Will, and rushed toward him. In a moment, she had her arms wrapped around him, and they kissed as though their lives depended on it. In many ways, they did. Ella's eyes were closed tightly; all she could feel were his pillow-soft lips and the urgent grip of his powerful hands, and the way his heart thudded against her chest as they pressed against each other.

They kissed like this for a breathless ten minutes, at least. When they came up for air, they locked eyes, totally speechless. Ella had thought they would never kiss again. Now, here they were, lost in one another's embrace.

"I..." Will began to speak but soon abandoned it. "I'm sorry. I don't know what to say."

"I don't, either." Slowly, Ella shifted off of Will's lap and straightened her hair. Her heart ballooned with love for him. *Say something. Tell him you love him.* But she couldn't bring herself to do it. She was overwhelmed with fear.

Finally, Ella lifted her eyes back toward the shelf, which pointed down toward the ground. The photographs and trophies on that shelf had fallen to the ground. Ella stepped toward them, picking them up one by one and piling them up on a side desk. Then she glanced up at where the shelf had disconnected from the wall.

There, where the shelf had been connected, was a small hole in the wall.

"That's weird." Ella stepped closer, peering into the wall from below. "Will? Can you think of any reason why someone would hang a shelf like this?"

Will's eyes were at a great distance, as though he remained in shock after the kiss. He strode toward the hole in the wall, which he could peer directly into, given his height. "There's something in there." A split second later, he procured what looked like a very dusty book, then handed it down to Ella.

"Huh." Ella was at a loss. She blew across the book so that dust sprinkled toward the ground. It was a black leather journal tied up with two leather strings. The corners of her lips twisted into a smile as she said, "I wonder if it's a map to buried treasure?"

Will appreciated the joke, chuckling as he swung his fingers through his hair. His eyes still echoed with love for her. Did she deserve it? *Did either of them deserve a second chance after all they'd thrown away?*

Ella leaned against the desk in the practice room and slowly wound the leather strings from the journal to open it. "What will we do with the buried treasure?" She wanted to be playful and light. Maybe that way, they wouldn't have to discuss what the kiss had meant.

"Maybe we could buy every famous guitar in the world," Will suggested.

"Oh. Great idea." Ella laughed nervously. "We could finally buy Prince's Cloud Guitar."

"The one he used in Purple Rain?"

"The very one."

Will wagged his eyebrows. "Lofty goals."

Ella grinned madly, then opened the journal to the very middle. "Buried treasure, here we come."

The moment Ella began to read the writing within, however, all the blood drained from her cheeks. "What is this?"

The page Ella had turned to was a very long list of what looked to be character traits.

- **Loves golf. Plays Tuesdays, Thursdays, and Saturdays at Siasconset.**
- **Has three children - Kendall, Charity, and Roy.**
- **NOTE: He is not currently speaking with Roy because he doesn't approve of Roy's wife.**
- **ALWAYS compliment his dog. Name: Ruthie.**

Ella parsed through her mind for some understanding of this. "This is so weird," she muttered. "It's a list of stuff about one of my father's best friends and colleagues back in the day, Marvin Hallmark. He had this dog named Ruthie that he took with him absolutely everywhere. And I remember the scandal when his son married someone he didn't like. My dad said that Marvin swore he would never talk to Roy again."

Ella turned the book so that Will could see the list, which continued to the next page. At the very end of the list, the same person had written the words:

BANK DETAILS: still working

"What the heck?" Ella hissed, her eyes flashing.

"What do the other pages say?" Will asked.

Ella continued to flip through the pages to find more details about various colleagues and ex-friends of her father. Gregory Puck's list included: **REMEMBER that he LOVES when you flirt with him in front of his wife.** Under a female friend's list was written: **Feminist to a**

**fault. Perhaps hint that you went to a pro-choice
rally in college.** Another man was listed as: **HUNGRY for
an affair. Make him think that he can have it with
you.** Some of the names had bank details listed, which had
surely been difficult to get.

Ella's heart thudded with a mix of fear and intrigue.
Slowly, she flipped toward the very front of the journal, where
she found the words **BERNARD COPPERFIELD** scribed
in big, bold lettering. Around the name, someone had drawn
little hearts.

"It's like a maniacal schoolgirl wrote this," Ella
breathed.

"What does your dad's list say?" Will asked, his eyes
buggy.

Ella's eyes watered. "I don't even know if I want to read
it."

Will placed a hand on her shoulder and squeezed it
gently. "I'm right here. It's okay. You can do this."

Ella nodded, sniffed, and forced her eyes back to the
page.

- **Absolutely obsessed with his time in
  Paris, where he met his wife (GRETA)**
- **Greta is much smarter than she looks—
  be wary of her at all times.**
- **Bernard is INCREDIBLY well-connected
  — in the literary, film, and music
  worlds.**
- **Friends in all corners of the world with
  very deep bank accounts. $$$**
- **Children: Quentin, Alana, and Julia**
- **In a moment of drunk sorrow, Bernard
  told you that his youngest, Ella, was**

adopted after her mother abandoned her at The Copperfield House.
- **This adoption is a secret that both Bernard and Greta carry. USE THIS to your advantage, if you can.**

Ella felt as though her body had caught on fire. She dropped the leather journal and leaped back, her legs and arms shaking violently. "Oh my God. Oh my God." She repeated it over and over, overwhelmed. Will bent to pick up the leather book and read over Bernard's first page before whispering, "There are twenty pages about Bernard."

"And the rest of the book is all about his friends and colleagues," Ella rasped. "She was studying him. She was making lists. She was maniacal about it." She cupped her elbows like a child, overwhelmed. "I don't know what to say."

"This is the book of a sociopath," Will said firmly, closing it.

Ella's eyes widened as the realization flowed over her. "It's Marcia. It has to be."

Will set his jaw. For a moment, Ella was afraid that he would refute this idea and come up with another. Instead, he said, "How can you be sure?"

Ella collapsed on the seat in front of the drum set and closed her eyes. "Marcia knew about my real mother. It all makes sense now." She shuddered, then explained, "I had this feeling that she was chasing after me. She'd gone out drinking with you, she'd purchased the painting of Alana, and she'd decided to premiere her film at the Nantucket Jubilee. I was so angry, and I sent a message directly to her website, telling her to stay away from my family. The next thing I knew..."

"You learned about your real mother?" Will finished, catching on.

Ella's vision was foggy with tears. After a moment of

terribly tense silence, she whispered, "But this is proof, Will. Real proof."

Will continued to flip through the pages, flabbergasted. "She never signed her name."

"There has to be a way to show it's hers." Determination flowed through Ella. Anger was such a powerful tool. "I'll talk to Alana and Julia about it. Together, we'll come up with a plan."

Chapter Twenty

S leep didn't come for the Copperfield Sisters easily that
night. After Ella showed the journal to Alana and Julia,
they were breathless with anger, reading through the
lists with dangerous tones. They meant business. Bit by bit,
they crafted a plan for Marcia's arrival on the island— one that,
if it worked well, could begin to unravel the "beautiful" life that
Marcia had built for herself. They wanted to put her in prison
for many years, to pay the same price that Bernard had. If they
couldn't, then ruining her prestige would have to do. When
they finally convinced one another to go to bed, they held one
another for a long time, unable to weep any longer. Again, both
Alana and Julia reminded Ella that she was just as much a
Copperfield as any of them were— and Ella finally said, "I
know."

The following early afternoon was the opening ceremony
of the Nantucket Jubilee. Ella arrived downtown at eleven to
find Stephanie in a rather bouncy and good mood.

"We've prepared for everything we can," Stephanie
explained. "If something goes wrong, that is out of our control."

This was such a contrast to the Stephanie of the previous several weeks, who hadn't been able to get through a meeting without a mid-grade panic attack. Ella hugged her and said, "You've done such a remarkable job, Steph. Thank you for including me in the process."

To start the festivities, a large sailboat styled like an old-fashioned whaling boat entered the harbor. On shore, multiple Nantucketers in 1820s-style costumes waved and cried out excitedly. Ella, Julia, and Alana watched from the docks, laughing at how silly and also how beautiful the re-enactment actually was.

Several Nantucketers had speaking parts. One woman screeched, "Is that The Heart of Nantucket?"

Another woman cried, "I thought the ocean had taken our men forever!"

A teenage girl wept, "My father! He's finally home!"

Ella, Alana, and Julia chuckled at the bad acting yet were just as quiet as everyone else as the sailboat was latched to the main dock and a number of "whalers" stepped off, also in 1820s clothing. One of the men raced off the dock, lifted his real-life wife into the air, and kissed her right in front of everyone. Their real-life teenagers stood further to the back, all in ordinary clothing, and they wrinkled their noses with shame.

Still, Ella had to admit that it was all rather sweet. The re-enactment showed the true heart of Nantucket. Everyone was overly willing to go the extra mile to prove their love for their home. That was a rare thing in the world.

After the re-enactment, Stephanie made a speech on the little stage next to the harbor. Her voice wavered slightly, but she powered through, thanking the numerous musicians, film-makers, writers, and other performers for their commitment to Nantucket. "The Nantucket Jubilee celebrates two hundred years of homecomings," she explained, her smile widening. "And I couldn't have put any of this together without another homecoming, one that's a bit more personal to me." Stephanie exhaled deeply and laughed. "I hope I don't start sobbing. Gosh. Okay. My best friend in the world left the island when we were eighteen. Two months ago, she came back and threw her heart and mind into the Nantucket Jubilee like no other. Ella Copperfield, thank you. Thank you for coming back. I love you."

Ella's heart raced. She pressed her lips onto her palm and blew a kiss toward Stephanie, who caught it in her fist and laughed. She then added, "Enough about me. Let's kick off this celebration, shall we? First up, we have local band, The Scavengers, to play you jazz and blues hits. There are food trucks lined up all over the place, plenty of games and prizes to win, and what looks to be about a million pies to eat. I hope you're hungry. Let's celebrate!" Stephanie flung her hand into the air and laughed joyously. The crowd joined her, applauding and separating to line up at food trucks and little wine stalls. The local band, The Scavengers, marched on stage and began to tune their instruments as Alana said, "I think we all deserve a glass of wine after what happened last night."

As Ella, Alana, and Julia sat around a little wooden table, each with a glass of natural wine, Stephanie appeared to give Ella a walkie-talkie, "just in case." "We worked tirelessly, and every extra employee we hired is currently in place," Stephanie explained. "But if there's any hiccup in the plan, I'll contact you here, and we can hit up Plan B or Plan C."

Ella saluted Stephanie. "We got this."

As The Scavengers played and the three sisters sipped their wine, they spotted several Nantucketers in the crowd who'd been listed in Marcia's horrible leather journal. Ex-colleagues and ex-friends of Bernard walked around with natural wines and locally brewed beers, each with a smile on their face.

"It's so strange," Ella whispered. "Twenty-five years ago, these people lost millions of dollars."

"Most of them got it back with insurance," Julia pointed out.

"And they were able to get over it by demonizing our father," Alana said. "Everyone needs a scapegoat."

"He was an easy target," Ella breathed. "All roads pointed back to him."

"And now, all roads point back to this journal," Alana affirmed. "Jeremy's already confirmed that he can help us tomorrow. His handwriting analyst will be at-the-ready. You said that she gets in around one?"

"That's right," Ella said. "According to her personal assistant, she plans to check in at the Nantucket Community Music Center before heading to wherever she's staying."

"I hate the idea that she has a private residence on Nantucket," Alana muttered.

"I'm pretty sure she does. How else did she maintain a friendship with Gregory Puck all these years?" Ella said, remembering that Gregory had agreed to make a speech before Marcia's film premier.

"For twenty-five years, the four of us and Dad didn't have anything to do with the island," Julia muttered angrily. "But she was allowed to traipse around, use her money for whatever she pleased, and basically make the island her own."

"I can't stand it," Ella breathed.

For a moment, they held the silence. All of them brimmed with fear and hope for the following day.

"Oh, look! There's Danny and Will." Julia's smile brightened as she pointed out across the crowd.

Sure enough, Danny and Will walked side-by-side along with a number of Danny's teammates from the football team. Will and Danny looked confident and easy as they bantered, each with a coke in hand. Ella's heart swelled with love for them.

"So. You and Will were in the practice room last night?" Alana asked mischievously.

Ella rolled her eyes, sensing where Alana wanted to take the conversation. "We just wanted to play some of our old songs to see if we still could."

"And? Did you find that old, sweet rhythm?" Julia teased.

"Julia!" Ella hissed, feeling as silly and vibrant as a teenage girl in love.

"Oh my gosh. Something happened," Alana whispered. "I would recognize Ella's 'lying face' anywhere."

"I'm not lying," Ella lied, searching through her mind for any other subject. After a moment, however, a spontaneous smile burst across her face. She'd given herself away. "I swear! I'm not lying!" she lied again as she shivered with laughter.

Julia rubbed Ella's shoulder lovingly and said, "Yeah, yeah. We believe you," in a sarcastic tone.

"You guys are such 'older sisters,'" Ella said, heaving a sigh. "What the heck would I do without you?"

* * *

The following afternoon at twelve-thirty, Ella, Alana, and Julia sat in stunned silence in the small office directly beside the main foyer in the Nantucket Community Music Center. Only moments before, Marcia Conrad's personal assistant had texted Stephanie and Julia to say that Marcia was "right on time and ready for the big day." It felt as though a hurricane was headed straight toward them, threatening to destroy everything they'd newly built that summer. Marcia certainly had a good track record for ruining their lives.

"Just make sure I don't storm out there and start screaming," Ella muttered under her breath. "It would blow our cover."

"If you do, I'll be right behind you," Julia affirmed.

"Me, too," Alana said.

They held the silence again. Ella blinked back anxious tears, then muttered, "I just hate the fact that I would never have known about my real mother if it wasn't for her."

Julia squeezed Ella's elbow kindly and tilted her head. "She wanted to use that information to manipulate you and control you. Now, we're using her own manipulation tactics against her. It's invigorating."

"But nobody's blaming you for feeling complicated about your real mother," Alana affirmed. "Least of all, our own mother. I've hardly seen her this week."

"She's keeping a low profile," Julia affirmed. "I know the guilt is eating her alive."

Ella nodded sorrowfully. "I just haven't known what to say. But once this is over with Marcia, I'll find a way to talk to her. I have to." She sighed, then added, "She's the only mother I've ever known. I've loved her, and I've hated her, and I've missed her, and I've..."

"Felt every feeling imaginable toward her?" Julia asked. "Then I guess she's really your mother."

Marcia Conrad appeared in the foyer of the Nantucket Community Music Center at twelve-fifty-seven. According to several blogs and articles Ella had read about Marcia, Marcia ascribed to the sentiment that "to be early means to be on time." From the little window between the office and the main foyer, Ella peered out to see a remarkably "money-ed" woman with blond blown-out curls, iconic Louboutin heels, a dress that showed off her impressive fifty-something cleavage, and a cinched waist. She greeted Stephanie at the front desk with a plastic smile.

"Good afternoon, Ms. Conrad!" Stephanie said joyously. "Thank you for your commitment to our little island."

Marcia Conrad spoke quietly, maintaining piercing eye contact. She then bent down and began to read the questionnaire that the Copperfield Sisters had provided, with questions about what Nantucket meant to her, what her connection to Nantucket was, and how she felt her film represented Nantucket as a whole. Ella had asked Stephanie to explain that the questionnaire would be featured in an upcoming Nantucket literary magazine, which had a special focus on film. According to Jeremy's friend, the handwriting analyst, it was best to have a lot to work with; the more Marcia wrote, the better.

"I'd be glad to fill this out," Marcia murmured, shifting her weight on her heels as she flourished a pen across the questionnaire.

In the little office, Alana, Ella, and Julia remained breathless. For the first time since they'd concocted their scheme, she asked herself: *What if the handwriting wasn't a match? What if the journal was just a coincidence? Or what if the journal belonged to someone else entirely?*

Suddenly, the front door of the Nantucket Community Music Center opened to reveal none other than Will, who sauntered in off the street just as any handsome rock star would. Marcia turned swiftly and shrieked girlishly with surprise. Ella's jaw dropped as she stirred in a mix of jealousy and humor. After all, Will had known that Marcia would arrive just about now.

Obviously, Will wanted to mess with Marcia just a little bit.

"Will? My goodness! I had no idea that you were performing at the Nantucket Jubilee." Marcia tucked a blond strand behind her ear and flirted easily, like a high schooler.

Will's smile took Ella's breath away. Was it really possible that he was hers again?

"Marcia Conrad! I didn't know you'd be here, either. I guess I should pay better attention to my emails," Will teased.

"I use my assistant for that," Marcia quipped.

Will laughed joyously. Ella had to hand it to him; he was a pretty good actor.

"You'll have to come to my premier," Marcia continued. "Your song is featured multiple times throughout the film. I think you'll really love the way it's used."

Will's eyes widened. "With your artistic talent, I have no doubt."

Marcia giggled again. "Maybe we can meet for the after-party tonight."

"I wouldn't miss it for the world," Will affirmed.

Marcia waved her pen knowingly, then said, "I'll see you later, then," before returning her attention to the questionnaire. Will stepped through the foyer and walked directly through the door, behind which Ella remained hidden. When he was latched away with the three Copperfield Sisters, Ella burst into giggles that she struggled to keep quiet.

"You've got to be kidding me," she whispered. "You just wanted to keep her on her toes, didn't you?"

Will shrugged. "I just want her to be extra high up before she falls."

A few minutes later, after Marcia clicked her pen closed and returned to her limousine outside, Stephanie burst through the door of the little office, waving the questionnaire frantically.

"I got it!" she cried, grateful to be in on the Copperfield Sisters' scheme. "Let the games begin!"

Chapter Twenty-One

T he entirety of Nantucket's Main Street bustled with crowds, buzzed with local music and conversation, and came alive with the smells of countless food trucks and stalls— fish and chips, tacos, empanadas, and fried chicken, to name a few. Danny had reserved a table for the three of them directly next to the fish and chips stand on Main Street, where Main looped off to form Centre. As Ella and Will approached, hand-in-hand, Ella's heart pitter-pattered with excitement for this brand-new life they'd built together. Even now, the handwriting analyst studied Marcia's handwriting. Even now, they were closer than they'd ever been to righting every wrong.

Once Ella and Will reached the table at the fish and chips stand, Laura burst out from behind Danny and erupted with laughter. "Surprise!" she cried as she scrambled around the picnic table and threw her arms around her mother and father. Danny hugged them both, too, as they explained that they'd come up with the idea only a few days ago.

"Danny said that you've been working so hard on the

Nantucket Jubilee," Laura said, glowing with joy. "I knew I had to see what this was all about."

"What do you think so far?" Ella asked.

Laura's eyes widened. "It's incredible. The entire island feels so alive."

Laura returned to the picnic table and began to speak excitedly to Danny about something at Columbia. Will and Ella exchanged smiles as Will said, "I guess since we're the parents, it's up to us to buy the grub?"

"Parenting is expensive," Ella joked as they stepped toward the line at the fish and chips stand, studying the menu. "I guess we'd better get four servings."

"Maybe in a few years, they'll both be all grown up and making the kind of money we only ever dreamed about," Will said.

"Danny is a brilliant scientist and mathematician," Ella affirmed. "Who knows where he'll end up?"

A few people in front of them in line, a man in a red cap, had a great deal of trouble deciding what to order. He asked one question after another, humming and hawing as the fish and chips dealer struggled not to roll his eyes. Ella and Will exchanged glances and snickered. Will then took Ella's hand in his again as though it was an impulse.

Ella's lips opened in surprise. It was both exhilarating and so normal to hold Will's hand. Since Thursday night's discovery of the leather book (and the make-out session), they hadn't discussed where they stood with each other.

"Will..." Ella began, suddenly terrified.

Will spread his hand across her cheek and swept his thumb across her chin. His touch was so tender.

"Will, what are we doing?" Ella asked, her voice cracking.

"What do you think we're doing?" Will whispered so that nobody else in line for the fish and chips could hear.

Ella's eyes searched his. "Are we...?" She dared to ask him if they were back together, if this meant that they could restore their family, and if this meant that they would tour as Pottersville again.

Suddenly, Will removed a small velvet box from his pocket. As panic rolled through her, Ella stared at the box as though it was covered in acid. Then, her eyes lifted, Will and Ella stared at one another for a painfully long moment, neither speaking.

How many times had they told one another that they didn't "need" to get married like everyone else? How many times had they assured each other that they were happy enough?

Yet here they were on a Saturday afternoon in the middle of October, and Will had decided to pop the question.

Before Ella could find her voice, her phone buzzed with a call. Ella stuttered, grabbed the phone from her pocket, and answered, "Alana. Hey. What's up?" All the while, she maintained eye contact with Will, whose face evoked all the love in the world. Slowly, he slid the engagement ring back into his pocket, nodding. Ella's heart beat so quickly that she thought it might burst through her chest.

"Hey!" Alana sounded breathless. "He's analyzed the handwriting. I'm headed back to Main Street with a copy of his statement."

"Wow. What did he say?"

"It's a match!" Alana cried. "She's such a snake, Ella. Gosh, I can hardly handle my own anger right now."

"Ella!"

Another voice rang out from the crowd. Ella's stomach swirled with hunger and anxiety. Quickly, she turned to peer through the throngs of people for the source of the voice. Finally, the source of the voice, Julia, pushed through the crowd, her eyes frantic.

Behind Julia was a very familiar face. The sight of it sent shivers up and down Ella's spine. Her lips formed a round O, heavy with questions.

This man was the dark, arrogant, six-foot-three renowned public figure from all American television screens. This was Quentin Copperfield, a nightly news anchor based in New York City, and the elder brother all of them had begun to forget – if only because he'd separated himself so entirely from the rest of the family. Here he was, charging toward Ella with anger marred across his face.

Ella and Will quickly stepped out of the fish and chips line and prepared for Quentin's attack. Will's hand cupped Ella's elbow for support. Suddenly, both Julia and Quentin were upon them as Quentin growled, his eyes penetrating, "What in the hell have you done to Mom?"

"I tried to tell him that today isn't the day for this," Julia said, fiddling with the hair around her face. "There's too much going on. And besides, it's not like he knows the entire story."

Quentin bucked around, giving Julia another of his demonic expressions. "The only story I need to know is that our mother called me three times this week, crying so desperately that I could hardly make out what she said. Eventually, I heard the name, 'Ella,' and put two and two together." He spun back to glare at Ella as he demanded, "Did you storm back into that house and try to make our mother pay for everything that happened twenty-five years ago? Because that's cruel, Ella. She's an old woman." Quentin seethed, then added, "I told you both that we needed to move Mom down to New York City so that I could keep an eye on her. Nobody believed me. Now, she's at her wits' end. And here I am, taking another day away from my very important career to clean up yet another Copperfield mess."

Ella's jaw dropped. The sheer insanity of what he said shocked her. As Quentin huffed, Ella and Julia locked eyes in understanding.

"We need to talk," Ella said, her voice low and sinister.

Maybe it was something about her tone that made Quentin

nod his head, his nostrils flared. Sure, he would hear her out—but he wanted to let her know that he wasn't pleased about it.

"I don't have much time," Quentin affirmed. "I need to get back to The Copperfield House to see our mother."

"You can see her once we explain," Ella said simply. She then turned to meet Will's gaze, her heart lurching with regret. Only moments ago, Will had procured a little velvet box in preparation to pop the question that Ella had never thought she'd hear. How funny and tragic it was that they still couldn't get engaged, even when their hearts cried out for it.

"Will? You and the kids should stay here," Ella offered. "Eat some fish and chips and enjoy the concerts. Quentin, Julia, and I won't be too long."

Will placed a strong and tender hand across her shoulder. "Promise you're okay?"

Ella nodded. She placed her hand over his on her shoulder and breathed, "Everything will be fine." She said it because it had to be fine. There was no other way.

Julia led Ella and Quentin back across Main Street, walking out toward Nantucket Harbor. Around them, Nantucketers roamed with ice cream cones and hot dogs, wearing baseball hats and t-shirts that said: **THE HEART OF NANTUCKET 1822**. Ella and Stephanie had arranged that all the revenue for the baseball hats and t-shirts would go toward charity.

"Let's sit over there," Ella said, pointing toward a free picnic table alongside a natural wine stand.

Quentin sat, his face stoic and domineering. Julia and Ella waited in line to grab them all drinks, watching as several Nantucketers approached Quentin to shake his hand.

"We watch you every night of the week," a woman in her fifties told him.

"My wife says that you're the only news anchor she trusts," a man said, his eyes reflecting a mix of jealousy and euphoria.

"He's really something, isn't he?" Julia muttered under her breath.

"I can't believe he came all this way to yell at me," Ella offered. "Or, then again, it's Quentin. Of course, I can believe that."

Julia groaned and checked her phone. "Alana should be here in a few minutes. Maybe she can talk some sense into him."

"He always respected her more because of Asher," Ella muttered.

"You think he'll still respect her now that they're getting divorced?" Julia whispered.

"I don't know. To be honest, I've never understood Quentin. I've never understood his motivations, his thought processes, or any of his decisions. I don't think today will be any different," Ella returned.

By the time Alana arrived, Ella, Julia, and Quentin sat at the picnic table, each with a glass of still-untouched natural wine. Alana dropped a kiss on Quentin's cheek (something left-over from her European past) and sat down beside him. Quentin looked uncomfortable, as though he was accustomed to "lording over" other people due to his fame but had just remembered he couldn't do that very well with his sisters.

"Thanks for this," Alana said, breaking through the silence as she lifted the glass they'd gotten her. She then studied Quentin's profile, sipped the wine, and said, "So, Quentin. What's up?"

Quentin barked, "I've come here to take our mother back to the city once and for all. Obviously, you three can't care for her properly."

"Wait just a minute," Ella demanded, her anger growing.

"Right. Ella seems to think she has some information that I don't have," Quentin offered, rolling his eyes. "Out with it, Ella. What can you tell me to change my mind about your horrendous actions toward our mother? What could possibly excuse five phone calls from Greta Copperfield, all of which eventually led to her bursting into tears?"

Ella set her jaw. She just needed to come out with it and tell Quentin about the biggest event in her recent life as though she spoke about nothing at all, like the weather. In front of Quentin, she'd always wanted to seem stronger than she actually was. Today was no different.

"Greta and Bernard aren't my real parents. They never told me." Against her best wishes of confidence and strength, Ella's vision was suddenly blurry with tears. "I recently found out the truth, and I've needed time away from Greta to figure out what it means that she and Bernard lied to me for forty-two years."

As Ella spoke, Quentin's face was transformed. His sharp edges softened, his eyes dampened, and his shoulders slumped forward, proving him to be much less arrogant than he liked to appear. After a long moment, he whispered, "That's impossible."

"It's not," Ella said. "Greta confirmed it."

Quentin glanced toward Julia and Alana, who nodded in affirmation.

"My mother was staying at The Copperfield House in 1980," Ella continued, wanting to fill in the blanks. "She was a musician and terribly unprepared to be a mother. Greta said she would care for me just for a little while until my mother got on her feet. Unfortunately, she never heard from my mother again."

"And the lie got bigger and bigger," Quentin finished, understanding the weight of what his parents had done.

Quentin hung his head, his eyes closed. Alana placed a tender hand on his upper back and whispered, "We've told Ella over and over again that she's our sister, through and through."

"She's our sister," Quentin affirmed, his voice raspy.

"There's no question in my mind about that. But dammit, I can understand how painful it feels to learn that your life is not what you always assumed it to be."

Ella was taken aback at Quentin's sudden softness. She'd expected to have to fight him tooth and nail. Tentatively, she sipped her glass of wine and steadied her breath, grateful for this moment of calm.

"I have no intention of leaving Nantucket," Ella said suddenly, surprising herself. "And I have no intention of leaving Mom. Back when I was a teenager, Mom was my entire world. I did everything to make sure she ate and slept and kept herself alive. I also came back to Nantucket frequently over the years, so much so that Greta has always had something of a relationship with my children."

Quentin's eyes darkened with sorrow. After a dramatic pause, he muttered, "I know that Julia and I can't say the same about our children."

Ella lifted a shoulder. "I don't say this to pin the blame on anyone. On top of it all, hearing that our mother has called you sobbing all week tears me apart inside."

"Me too," Julia rasped. "Since I got back in April, I've felt that her mental health has improved by leaps and bounds."

"Her past came up to bite her," Alana whispered as her eyes found Ella's. "Yet again."

"I wish the Copperfields weren't continually slaves to our pasts," Ella muttered, her eyes to the table. "It's always one thing after another. With each new battle, I don't necessarily feel stronger. I just feel exhausted."

Julia placed her hand over Ella's on the picnic table. For a long time, the Copperfield siblings held the silence. Ella stewed in memories from 1997 of the last dinner they'd ever had as a family. Quentin had returned from Los Angeles, where he'd been cutting his teeth as an actor. Alana had visited from New York City, where she'd moved with Asher to become a model.

Only Julia and Ella had been at home, lost in the chaos of their separate teenage realities.

Marcia had been there, too. She'd been a youthful, blond spitfire, and she'd cast furtive looks at Bernard that made everyone believe that her love for him extended far beyond his mentorship.

Suddenly, a man in his sixties appeared at the table, gasping for breath. He held a little plate of tacos, and he looked at Quentin with watery yet childish eyes.

"Quentin Copperfield? Is that you?" the man asked.

The mood at the table couldn't have been worse. Tension hovered around them like a cloud. Quentin took a split second to readjust his face before he said, "It is, indeed. Just spending a bit of time with my family. I hope you enjoy the rest of the Nantucket Jubilee!"

The words were meant to end the interaction immediately, but the man didn't take the hint.

"I just loved that news segment you did the other night on the violence of New York City in the nineties," the man continued, rubbing his palms together. "It's like I always tell my wife; you don't just tell a story. You seem to paint a picture, drawing the viewer back into the folds of history."

"That's very kind of you." Quentin's voice remained stilted. He gave the stranger another nod, then waited another second more before he added, "Again, it's wonderful to hear from my viewers."

When the man finally headed away, Alana's nose shivered as she said, "I'd forgotten what it feels like to have your space invaded like that."

"I'm sure it used to happen to you and Asher all the time," Julia confirmed.

Alana nodded sadly. It wasn't clear if she felt nostalgic for this past or if she resented it. Perhaps she carried a bit of both.

Suddenly, Ella's posture stiffened. The non-stop

approaching fans of Quentin Copperfield had given her an idea, one that burned through the back of her skull.

"Alana, did you bring the journal back with you?"

Alana nodded, lifting her purse onto the table. "And I have the handwriting analyst's notes. A copy of them, anyway."

"Incredible," Ella breathed, filling her lungs.

"What is this about?" Quentin's question was sharp yet edged with curiosity.

Julia arched her left eyebrow and then muttered, "Show him," to Alana, who drew the leather book out of her purse and splayed it open to show Quentin, first, the terribly long list of Bernard's attributes, including information that could be used for blackmail. As Quentin read the list, his lips parted with shock and intrigue. By the time he reached the other names in the book— twenty-seven, all-told, all the color had drained from his cheeks.

At the perfect time, Alana flipped the brand-new questionnaire that Marcia had only just filled out from the inside of her purse. Even from where Ella sat, it was clear that the handwriting was the same; the questionnaire's handwriting just had a little less "youthful flair" to it.

"You've got to be kidding me," Quentin muttered, eyeing the name at the top of the questionnaire. Then, his eyes burning, he met first Alana's, then Julia's, then Ella's gaze. He rapped his finger against the leather binding of the book with zealous energy that didn't seem like it belonged to Quentin at all. "You've got her. You know that? You've really got her."

Ella's lips quivered into a smile. "I think I have an idea. Quentin, are you up for helping us?"

Quentin set his jaw. "Let me know what I can do."

Chapter Twenty-Two

Stephanie was initially tentative about Ella's plan. As she shuffled around the little office at the Nantucket Film Festival's main cinema, the Dreamland Film, Theatre, and Cultural Center, hunting for her list of film critics who planned to be at Marcia's premier that evening, she guffawed with worry. "So many people are coming here tonight to see this film, Ella," she said. "So many people are coming to hear Marcia Conrad speak!"

Ella's heart crackled at the edges. She crossed and uncrossed her arms as she said, "Stephanie, the Nantucket Jubilee has been such a tremendous success. You know that?"

Stephanie stopped short, lifting her eyes to Ella's. After a dramatic pause, she said, "It really has been wonderful, hasn't it?"

"But the thing about events like this is that the memories fade," Ella continued. "Unless there's a bit of drama. The kind of drama to write home about. The kind of drama that produces multiple think pieces, blog articles, and YouTube videos. If you go through with my plan, then I can almost guarantee that the

Nantucket Jubilee will be the talk of not only Nantucket but also the entire United States of America."

Stephanie's lips parted with surprise. As a small-town islander girl who'd hardly spent a lick of time off the island, the concept of this "entire United States" stopped her in her tracks.

"Besides, you can still premier Marcia's movie," Ella continued, pushing her luck. "It'll just come a few minutes late. That's all."

* * *

The premier for Marcia's new cinematic achievement, *Sweet Relief*, was set for eight o'clock that evening. Prior to the premiere, Ella returned to The Copperfield House to change into a black dress and style her hair. Julia, Alana, and Quentin were all at the house as well, speaking in excited whispers about their upcoming scheme. Already, Quentin was half-dressed in an Italian-cut suit, which he apparently always had on hand, "just in case."

After they dressed, the four Copperfield children sat on the back porch and watched the Nantucket waves roll toward the beach. Not far away, the Nantucket Jubilee soared on, its music floating through the air and permeating across the entire island.

"I talked to Mom this afternoon," Quentin said softly, avoiding his normal "authoritative" voice. "I told her that I know about your situation, Ella. And that I'm trying to understand the pain that you're all going through."

Ella's throat tightened.

"I invited her to come tonight," Quentin continued. "But because I couldn't explain what we were up to, I couldn't convince her to leave the house."

"Any sign of Dad?" Ella asked.

Quentin shook his head.

"He was better about making an appearance for a little while," Ella continued, swiping a tear from her eye.

"Healing from all we've been through has no timeline," Julia whispered.

They held the silence for a long time, all four of them wistful about the lives and dreams they could never get back and the parents that they would never fully know. Ella, too, was wistful about Joni Blackwood, wondering about the little personality details she might have inherited or if she'd have liked Ella and Will's music. Perhaps these thoughts would forever remain, tearing a hole in Ella's heart.

That night, Ella, Quentin, and Alana sat in the little room above the Dreamland Theatre, from which the projector illuminated the screen for hundreds of guests. Directly beside the traditional film projector, the Copperfield children had set up a digital film projector, which would allow them to project their newly created film, which Quentin had been able to film in a single take. As he was so experienced in the field of journalism, he'd been able to instruct Alana, Julia, and Ella on where to position the camera, how to set the lights, and when to cut the take. It had taken them little more than forty-five minutes to complete.

Now, their plan was in place.

"The theater is packed," Ella breathed, peering through the window at the hundreds of little heads down below. In the front row and off to the right, a blond woman sat by herself, one perfect leg crossed over the other. "I can see Marcia."

"Let me see." Alana leaped to the window to peer down at the beautiful woman who'd ruined their lives. "I don't think I've ever hated anyone more than I hate her right now," Alana rasped, which was saying something. Alana had met a lot of horrendous people.

Quentin, who'd loosened his tie and removed his suit jacket

after their first take, sat in the back of the projector room and nursed a beer. He looked both determined and pleased with himself. Julia stood off to the side, her arms crossed nervously over her chest. It wasn't clear if their scheme would work. Just then, it was all they had.

"We can't let her just parade in here and show off her movie like this," Julia muttered angrily. "She thinks she owns Nantucket Island, but she's wrong."

Suddenly, Stephanie appeared on the theater stage, her heels clicking as she walked to the center. Once she reached the podium, the crowd quieted in expectation. Ella had instructed Stephanie to say just what she'd planned to say, as though she hadn't any idea what would happen next. (Truthfully, Ella hadn't given Stephanie much to go on in terms of "what she was up to," anyway.)

"Good evening, ladies and gentlemen, and welcome to the first annual Nantucket Film Festival. My name is Stephanie Grayson, and it's been a unique pleasure to organize the Nantucket Jubilee from the ground up. Well, I say it's been a unique pleasure— but it's also been a whole lot of other things. A headache. A huge emotional obligation. A reason to cry at night."

The crowd ate out of Stephanie's palm, laughing joyously as her face lightened up. Ella laughed, too, grateful for this best friend from years ago and her continued commitment to Ella, the Island of Nantucket, and the rest of the Copperfield Clan.

"When I first learned that the great Marcia Conrad herself wanted to premier her film here at the Nantucket Film Festival, I nearly fell over," Stephanie continued to poke fun at herself. "After all, Marcia Conrad's list of accomplishments are about a mile long. She's paved the way for women in the film and literature industries, daring to dream impossible dreams. I can certainly say that when I was a little girl, I didn't think that women could be directors. To me, and to so many others, that was a man's job. Thank you, Ms. Conrad, for being a part of the wave of feminine influence that has proven me and so many others wrong."

The crowd applauded yet again. Ella's heart shivered with fear.

"Imagine my surprise to learn that Marcia Conrad has a very long history with Nantucket Island," Stephanie continued. "Years and years ago, she got her start at a once-beloved artist residency called The Copperfield House. Since then, she's summered here on Nantucket, building a lifelong commitment to the island and its mysticisms that will assuredly never go away. Now, without further ado, I'd like to introduce Marcia Conrad— who will introduce her stunning film herself."

The crowd roared so much that the glass in the window of the projector room shook. Ella leaped to attention, pressing the ON button of the projector, which required about thirty seconds to start up. As the crowd quieted, Marcia's voice swelled from the microphone.

"Thank you. Thank you." She paused for dramatic effect, then added, "I can't tell you how pleased I am to introduce my film at the Nantucket Film Festival. As Stephanie said, my love for Nantucket has been essentially lifelong. The first time I stepped off the ferry to land here, the island took my breath away. Since then, every time I've returned here, it's been a bit like returning home."

Suddenly, the projector flashed up on the screen directly behind Marcia so that a small shadow of her body appeared at the very bottom.

"Oh. Um?" Marcia placed her hand on her forehead, as though she shielded the sun. She spoke to the projector room as she said, "Could you guys give us a few more minutes? I have a few more things to say, and then my dear friend Gregory Puck has agreed to say a few words as well." She then returned her attention to the crowd to add, "The projection room is getting ahead of itself. I guess they want to get home early."

The crowd laughed knowingly, as though technology people were always "getting everything wrong."

But a split-second later, Quentin Copperfield's well-known mug appeared on the very large theater screen. In the film, he sat at a desk that mocked the desk that he normally sat at during his nightly news segment, and he adjusted a stack of papers, just as he normally did on television.

"Good evening," Quentin began.

Marcia began to speak into the microphone. "What is going on?" But midway through, someone cut her microphone. (Ella had a hunch that Stephanie had done it. She thanked her lucky stars for that.)

"My name is Quentin Copperfield. Perhaps you recognize me from my nightly news segment on Channel Four, where I've been delivering both local and national news for the better part of twenty years. Tonight, I'm streaming directly to the Nantucket Dreamland Theatre, which is a cinema that is very near and dear to my heart. You see, I was born and raised on Nantucket Island, where I was a part of the well-respected and much-adored Copperfield Family. As many of you— and certainly everyone in the Nantucket community— know, my father, renowned novelist Bernard Copperfield, was sentenced to twenty-five years in prison for stealing, swindling, and conning millions of dollars from his dearest friends and literary colleagues. Just last spring, he was released— but he did not return to a world he'd once known. In fact, since his sentencing, myself and my three siblings have held the belief that he was very much guilty of his crimes. It seemed clear to us. Until now."

On stage, Marcia swung her arms wildly over her head and screeched without the microphone's help. "Someone! Turn this off! What is going on!"

But the thing of it was, Quentin Copperfield was one of the most respected TV journalists across the United States. When Quentin started to speak, the world shut up to listen. This was no different. They were eating out of his hand.

On the screen, Quentin began to outline everything that Alana, Julia, and Ella had discovered since their return to The Copperfield House that spring. He discussed Alana's painting, Marcia's purchasing of Ella and Will's music for her film, and the emails that Bernard had supposedly sent to the friends he'd conned, which Marcia had seemingly echoed in a book she'd published much later.

"But on top of all of this evidence," Quentin continued. "The Copperfield Family discovered a leather-bound journal that seems to have been instrumental in manipulating and stealing from up to twenty-seven people." On-screen, Quentin procured the journal and opened it to read. "For example, midway through the journal, the owner has created a list for one Gregory Puck, a well-respected writer and philanthropist on the Island of Nantucket, and a man who my father cared for deeply.

"The journal says this. 'Remember, Gregory Puck, LOVES when you flirt with him in front of his wife. His favorite things to talk about include his literary achievements and the many girls he dated back in college.'" Quentin lifted his eyes back to the camera; his face tightened angrily. He then went on to read tidbits of lists from the rest of the journal, creating a portrait of a person who was borderline sociopathic.

"Is Marcia still here?" Ella whispered, eyeing the stage.

"I think she ran out!" Julia cried.

Ella's heart banged around in her chest. "I guess I wouldn't have expected her to hang around."

"There are so many journalists here," Julia murmured. "Marcia's name will be smeared through the mud by Monday morning."

"Gosh, I hope so," Ella breathed.

Quentin's video finished soon after, with Quentin saying, "Thank you for your attention this evening. This matter is of utmost importance not only to my family and I but also to the literary and film communities. If we allow such a person to lie and scheme her way to the top, then what else are we, as a society, capable of? We must protect ourselves from such attacks—and we must honor a great man who was terribly wronged. This is Quentin Copperfield with the nightly news. Thank you, and goodnight."

"You killed it, Quentin," Alana muttered.

As the lights turned back on below, the Nantucket Dreamland Theatre roared with gossip. Several people stood and began to take as many photographs of Stephanie, the stage, and the newly illuminated crowd as they could. Marcia was nowhere to be found, although many people howled, "Where is Marcia? We need a comment from Ms. Conrad herself!"

Ella continued to peer down at the cinema from on high, her ears roaring with the success of what they'd done. There was no telling what would happen next, yet it seemed clear that they were well on their way to righting the wrongs that had occurred more than twenty-five years ago.

Chapter Twenty-Three

That night at nine o'clock sharp, only one hour after Quentin Copperfield's news segment was broadcasted to a room of only a couple of hundred viewers, a film critic named Thomas Winston posted his own video of Quentin's speech, along with his own take on the matter. To finish, Thomas said, "It's this film critic and journalist's opinion that another set of eyes should be drawn to the 1997 issue of Massachusetts versus Bernard Copperfield. Perhaps justice was not served correctly. And perhaps we now have reason to believe that feminist film legend Marcia Conrad is to blame for millions of dollars in stolen funds."

"This is fantastic," Alana muttered as the Copperfield children watched the segment, which was well on its way to trending on social media. "How many followers does he have?"

"Almost a million," Julia said, her eyes flashing. "Gosh, journalists move quickly these days."

"We have to," Quentin affirmed, pouring himself a glass of wine as he shook his head in disbelief. "If this thing has the traction that I believe it to have, it should reach the entire United States by Monday."

The Copperfield children had returned to The Copperfield House immediately after the failed premier at the Nantucket Film Festival, brimming with expectation for what was to come. As a contrast, The Copperfield House was very quiet and dark, proof that both Greta and Bernard no longer lived in the world they'd once loved. It was up to the Copperfield children to bring them back.

"We should show this to Dad," Ella said softly. "He needs to know that the world's opinion of him is turning on a dime."

Julia's eyes traced toward the circular staircase that led up to his side of the house. "I'm sure he's still awake. Let me go see if he'll come downstairs for a little while."

It was best that Julia went to retrieve him, as they'd built up a more powerful father-daughter relationship since her return in April. This, Ella knew, was due to the fact that Julia had helped edit and restructure Bernard's book, which was a very intimate process that had united their hearts and minds. In any case, if anyone would convince him to come downstairs, it was Julia.

Next came the sounds of bombs. Ella leaped from her chair in surprise, watching out the window as the first of what would be a forty-five-minute firework show exploded across the water in a flurry of reds, blues, pinks, and yellows. Ella pressed her hand over her heart, enthralled with their beauty and their danger. Stephanie had said of this moment, "I need a 'wow' factor that shows the people of Nantucket just how important this Jubilee really is."

Alana suggested that they head out to the back porch so that they could see the fireworks display better. Quentin collected the bottle of wine while Alana and Ella grabbed blankets and sweaters from a little trunk in the living room. A moment later, they were bundled up on the back porch, watching the display. It was just as though they were children, sitting out on the back porch of The Copperfield House while their mother made them hot chocolate in the kitchen. How Ella yearned for those long-lost years. How strange to know that, in actuality, that family hadn't been her real family— and yet it was the only one she'd ever known.

"Quite a show out there." Bernard's voice boomed across the porch and echoed out across the beach. Ella whipped around to see him in his full glory: broad shoulders, scraggly beard, and somber eyes that seemed to carry the weight of all the horrible things he'd seen since 1997. Julia stepped in behind Bernard, looking anxious. Maybe she'd had to beg him to come.

"Dad." Alana rushed to her feet, allowing the blanket to fall. "We have something to show you."

Bernard sat between Alana and Ella while Julia and Quentin peered at them anxiously from the other side of the porch table. Out across the water, the fireworks continued to explode, producing a strange and volatile soundtrack. Alana played the video that they'd recorded of Quentin, along with the analysis from the famous film critic with nearly a million social media followers.

Bernard's face hardly registered what he saw. When it was over, he leaned back and placed his pipe tenderly between his lips, although he made no motion to light up. His eyes became distant, studying the explosions through the night sky.

"Don't you see, Dad?" Alana stuttered. "The world understands, now. They know that you didn't commit those crimes. That you're not this evil villain they've made you out to be."

"It's just like you said in your book," Julia continued quickly. "Now, people will put two-and-two together and recognize that you were always just the greatest man, incapable of hurting people in this way."

Quentin remained silent, as did Ella. Ella continued to

struggle to understand her father's facial expression. Had she expected him to leap up with joy? Had she expected him to thank them copiously for all they'd done?

Finally, Bernard spoke with quiet purpose. "I'm an old man, now. And as an old man, I find myself incapable of caring what anyone thinks of me. I just want my children to know that I would have never done anything that would have destroyed my family. I never would have done anything purposefully to break us apart."

Ella, Julia, Alana, and Quentin stared at the ground in shame, overwhelmed with the honesty in his words. Ella swam with sorrow and guilt. *Why had they been so quick to believe everyone else's opinion of Bernard? Hadn't Bernard only ever been the very best father, husband, and friend? Hadn't he always displayed himself to be endlessly empathetic, kind, intelligent, and forward-thinking?* Those sorts of men didn't commit crimes like this. Those sorts of men weren't guilty.

"I'm so sorry that I didn't believe in you, Dad." Quentin spoke first, surprising all of them. "I ran away from this family as quickly as I could, wanting to distance myself. I'll never forgive myself."

"I won't forgive myself, either," Julia stuttered.

"Me neither," Alana finished.

Ella's throat was so tight that it was difficult to swallow. Her eyes met her father's as her stomach twisted with rage at all the time they couldn't get back. "The fact that we didn't believe in you will haunt us forever." Ella thought again of the letters that Bernard had sent, which she'd hidden from her mother to try to keep Greta's mental health intact. How ashamed she now was of doing that!

But Bernard shook his head with disdain. On high, an enormous turquoise firework blasted through the clouds and illuminated the Nantucket Sound below.

"We can only move forward," Bernard whispered. "I hope we can do that together as a family."

After that, the four Copperfield children and their father sat in stunned silence, watching the rest of the firework display as it carried on till eleven at night. Time passed strangely, as though each of them were heavy with their own nostalgia and stirring through memories. When the firework display finished, they each went to bed with a quiet "Goodnight," their eyes shadowed with sorrow.

But that night, as Ella crawled into bed next to a sleeping Will for the first time in many, many months, Alana texted her.

ALANA: Check Twitter. Now.

Ella did. And there, under TRENDING, sat the words: #JusticeForBernard.

Chills crept along Ella's arms and legs. She pressed her phone against her chest and stared into the darkness as Will breathed in and out, dropping through dreamland. There was no telling what would happen next. Here she and the rest of the Copperfields sat, on the precipice of everything else.

Chapter Twenty-Four

Things on the internet moved quickly, just as they always did. By Monday morning, news of "the disaster at the Nantucket Film Festival" had reached multiple news channels, and Quentin's video had been shared nearly two million times. This renewed interest in Bernard's case had led "real internet trolls" (Laura's words, not Ella's) to dig deep into the dealings of Marcia Conrad, namely from the years 1997 and 1998. These so-called "internet trolls" had resources that the Copperfield children couldn't have dreamed of and soon pinned down Marcia's whereabouts and "inconsistent spending patterns."

According to several internet crusaders, Marcia had made several enormous payments between the years 1997 and 1998, during which time she funded her first film, funded her own film production company, Femme Fatale, and bought a house near the beach in Los Angeles.

"It begs the question," one journalist on a talk show later that day began, "of where she got that money."

"And all of this was going on while her supposed mentor

and dear friend, Bernard, was on trial for stealing millions," another on the talk show returned.

"It's fishy, to say the least," the other finished. "What's the statute of limitations on something like this?"

"In the state of Massachusetts, larceny has a statute of limitations of six to ten years," the other said. "But given the enormous amount of funds and the powerful people she may have stolen from, shouldn't we expect a trial?"

"Not necessarily," the other said, her face marred with sorrow. "That said, Marcia Conrad's name has been tarnished. This morning, her PR rep released a statement that says, essentially, that Marcia is 'innocent until proven guilty.' I'd love to see her prove her innocence."

Alana, Julia, and Ella sat captivated in front of the television screen, watching this talk show discuss the intricacies of their family's horrific past. Julia had cooked them all grilled cheese sandwiches, and each sandwich lay, forgotten and cooling, as they stared forward at the screen.

A moment later, Quentin, who had returned to the city, called Alana. She put him on speaker so that everyone could hear.

"Hey! The station wants to do a feature on the case," Quentin said excitedly. Around him on the phone, you could hear the buzz and whir of New York City traffic. For the first time ever, this sound didn't make Ella jealous in the slightest. She was grateful to be on Nantucket.

"Wow. That's huge, Quentin," Alana said, her eyes buggy.

"Yeah. I know." Quentin allowed a beat to pass before he added, "Is he doing okay?"

The Copperfield Sisters exchanged glances.

"We haven't seen him since you left," Julia finally admitted. "I think it's all been overwhelming for him."

"I was afraid of that," Quentin said. "But Julia, book sales have rocketed. You must be excited."

"Yeah." Julia didn't sound as though she was in any way pleased about the monetary development. "People want to engage with the enormous story he told while he was in prison. Many readers are finding reflections of their own regrets and sorrows within the text. And more than that, people are writing the publishing house, talking about how they're coming around to the idea of rekindling their relationships with their own parents or siblings, all because of our story."

"Are you serious?" Quentin sounded flabbergasted.

"The fact that Dad might have had a hand in bringing so many families back together has to be the best part," Ella breathed.

Deep in the back of her mind, a small voice whispered: *and now, your family is back together, too.* Will had hardly left Ella's side since the night of the Nantucket Film Festival.

What everyone said was true. The fact that Bernard, this innocent man, had lost so much time with his loved ones was proof that you needed to cling to the ones you loved all the more. Already, Ella and Will had lost so much time; they couldn't afford to lose another second.

Later that week, Bernard was invited to hold a reading of his novel at the small downtown Nantucket Bookshop. News of this invitation went through the proper channels: from Stephanie to Ella, to Julia, and finally, to Bernard himself. Bernard "hummed and hawed" about the decision for a number of days before he eventually told Julia, "Why the heck not?"

Saturday, October 15th, was the day of the reading. That morning, Ella awoke before her sisters, Will, and Danny and padded downstairs to a sun-filled kitchen to find her father and mother seated across from one another at the kitchen table, a large folder placed between them. Neither of them spoke. It had been weeks since Ella had seen her father and mother together, and the sight made her freeze in the kitchen doorway with her heart in her throat. Their faces were etched with anxiety.

"Ella. Will you please sit down?" Greta found her voice and gestured toward the chair between them.

Ella wobbled to the chair, wanting to rub the sleep from her eyes yet resisting it. As she sat, Greta spread her wrinkled hands across the folder, exhaled all the air from her lungs, and said, "Your father and I hired a private investigator to track down the whereabouts of Joni Blackwood."

It was as though Greta had slipped a knife through Ella's chest. Ella gaped at her, realizing, suddenly, that Greta and Bernard had decided, yet again, to go behind her back, to know more about her reality than she'd ever known herself. This time, however, Ella felt too tired to be sad. They'd been through too much.

Slowly, Greta flipped open the first page of the folder to show several photographs, all of which featured a woman in her twenties and early thirties. In the photographs, Joni was dressed in all manner of "hippie garb," her sleeves flourishing as she spoke about something that seemed important to her, a guitar across her lap or attached to her neck. Each photograph illustrated the dramatic brilliance and tragedy of a woman who just simply hadn't been ready for Ella. Perhaps she never would have been ready for Ella. Could Ella really demonize her for that?

Greta's hand shook as she revealed a copy of a newspaper printout, which she placed wordlessly in front of Ella.

OBITUARY for JONI BLACKWOOD: During the afternoon of October 7, 1987, Joni Blackwood passed away in her beautiful home in Laurel Canyon. She is survived in death by her dog, Felix, and many friends, who will miss her soul and her songs terribly. God bless you, Joni!

Ella's heart dropped to the base of her stomach. She read and reread the obituary, feeling as though she looked at it from a great distance, as though her body was disconnected from her mind.

Suddenly, Bernard's hand stretched over her wrist. Ella lifted her eyes to meet his.

"We cannot apologize enough for never telling you about this beautiful soul," he said, his voice low. "Ella, I'm so, so sorry for keeping this from you. It has eaten me up inside for forty-two years."

"And me." Greta reached across the table and took Ella's other wrist. "I don't know if I'll ever forgive myself."

Ella blinked back tears, stirring in confusion. For a solid minute, she stared into the mysterious yet familiar face of Joni Blackwood, wondering how she might have died, if she'd ever been in love, or if she'd ever thought of her daughter so far across the continent.

"The private investigator discovered one last thing," Greta whispered as she lifted the folder to reveal a vinyl beneath. The cover of the vinyl featured Joni Blackwood in another hippie dress, seated on a wooden swing with her legs pointed beautifully into the air. The album was called:

Joni Blackwood's "Songs for Forgotten Lovers"

"The private investigator said that very few of these albums remain," Greta continued softly.

"It's incredible that he was able to track it down," Bernard affirmed. "She died not long after it was released, which stopped production in its tracks."

"There was talk that she would be somebody in the folk scene," Greta said. "Which makes sense to us."

"She was a unique talent," Bernard continued, his eyes glistening. "Your talent would have made her so proud, Ella. Your musicality and the fame that came later make so much sense."

"But they're also uniquely yours," Greta reminded her. "You are a different kind of musician."

Greta and Bernard's old record player sat in the library,

newly connected to a set of old-fashioned speakers that Julia had found in a Copperfield House closet. Danny, Will, and Laura had played records on the record player over the last weekend, going through Bernard and Greta's old collection for many hours as an October rain had pattered across the windowpanes.

Now, Ella, Greta, and Bernard sat around the record player and listened as, in some impossible era, Joni Blackwood strummed through the first guitar chords of a song that seemed to come straight from her soul.

"How can we know what comes next?" Joni sang, her voice crackling with nostalgia. *"How can we know what we'll be?"*

Bernard Copperfield's reading from *The Time He Lost* at the Nantucket Bookstore drew a crowd of thousands. Several news crews stood outside, their anchors lifting microphones to their lips as they spoke about the enormity of the situation. "After twenty-five years in prison, Bernard Copperfield is finally breaking his silence."

Ella, Will, Danny, Alana, Jeremy, Julia, Charlie, and Greta sat in the front row of the little collection of chairs in the bookstore while the rest of the thousands of people hovered outside, chanting Bernard's name. It was eerie to hear Bernard's name echoing out across Nantucket Harbor, as though, for decades, all these people had been waiting for him and him alone.

True to his professional nature, Bernard arrived, said a few kind words, performed his reading, and answered a few questions to the small number of people who'd managed to grab a seat. Throughout the reading, Ella's eyes smarted at the emotion behind his words. It was often difficult to imagine him, seated in prison day after day, scribing the details of his broken heart. Yet here those details were, and the world was finally ready to listen.

Afterward, Julia asked Bernard if he wanted to have a meet-and-greet with the fans who stood outside, waiting for him. To this, Bernard shook his head no. Exhaustion lined his eyes, even as a smile made his dimples deepen.

"I want to go back to The Copperfield House, Julia. I want to go home." He then peered around Julia to catch Greta's eye. Greta shared a secret smile before she dropped her gaze to the ground, overwhelmed.

"Hey, Mom." Danny popped over to hug Ella. "I'm going to head out to meet a couple of friends."

"Sounds good, Danny." Ella brightened her face and rubbed his back. "By the way, I'm really impressed with how much you supported your grandfather's innocence when we first got to the island. I wish I could say that I'd been just as sure."

Danny's smile was crooked, just as handsome as his father's. "You have to trust in family, Mom." He then waved toward Will, adding, "See you later, Dad?"

"Later, son." Will waved back as Danny walked out into the massive crowd, eager to celebrate the rest of his youth. Luckily, it seemed that Nantucket Island had softened him; he was no longer eager to push himself to the limits of alcohol. He was no longer willing to destroy himself.

Soon after, Julia helped Greta, Alana, and Bernard escape home, driving her SUV through the throngs of people and the chaos of the media circus back toward their familiar property along the Nantucket Sound. Ella and Will remained at the outskirts of the masses, listening to the hum of conversation and watching as the media trucks packed up and raced away. It was chilly, in the low fifties, and the air hummed with expectation for the approaching winter.

Wordless and filled with emotion, Ella and Will wandered

toward the docks and hung their arms over the railing. The wind off the bay ripped across their faces and toyed with their hair. *How many years ago had they met, by then?* It seemed they'd lived enough stories to fill millions of years.

Finally, Ella found the strength to speak.

"I guess you head back on tour soon, don't you?" She had to find a way to be okay with it. She had to find a way through the pain of letting him go.

But Will just shook his head. "I told you. Touring and making music isn't the same without you. I canceled the rest of the tour."

Ella's eyes widened with surprise. She leaped back, watching his face for some sign of a joke. "You're kidding."

"I'm not." Will shook his head and turned to face her. He then took one of her hands in his as he reached into his pocket to remove a velvet box.

"Will..." Ella's voice was filled with disbelief. As he hadn't said anything about the velvet box since the previous weekend, she'd decided that maybe, it had all been in her head. Maybe he didn't want to marry her after all.

"Listen, Ella. I want to stay with you. I want to be with you. I want to raise Danny until graduation with you. But most of all, I want to marry you." He closed his eyes tenderly as he opened the velvet box, as though the emotion was too over-whelming to allow him to look her straight in the face.

The ring itself was a vintage diamond with a gold band, a simple yet sophisticated look that suited Ella, who wasn't so keen on "big jewelry."

Slowly, Will knelt to one knee, peered into her eyes, and whispered the words Ella had never imagined he would say.

"Ella. Will you marry me?"

"I've never wanted anything more. Yes, Will. I'll marry you."

Overcome with emotion, Will leaped from the ground,

wrapped his arms around her waist, and twirled her in a circle. Her cries of joy echoed out across the bay and the rest of the Nantucket Sound. Since Ella had been eighteen, Will had been her love, her music, her joy, her solace, and her rock. Why would an engagement ring change all that? What had they been afraid of all this time?

As they fell into their first of many kisses as fiancé and fiancée, Ella's heart pounded with expectation. The only fear she had was for a life without Will. "Till death do us part" were the only words that represented her love enough. Very soon, in front of God, her family, the government, and everyone else, they would become one.

Coming Next

Coming Next in the Nantucket Sunset Series

Pre Order From Nantucket, With Love

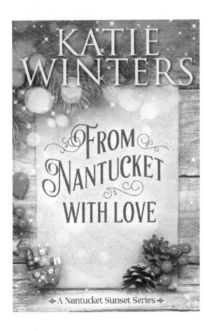

Other Books by Katie

Connect with Katie Winters

BookBub
Facebook
Newsletter

To receive exclusive updates from Katie Winters please sign up
to be on her Newsletter!

Made in the USA
Monee, IL
05 May 2023

33116251R10109